Freddy's back and everyone's cheering!

FREDDY THE DETECTIVE

One hilarious situation follows another as Freddy sets out to solve a series of mysteries on the Bean Farm—the Case of the Armored Train, the Case of Prinny's Dinner, the Mystery of Egbert. As Freddy says:

> "Oh, I am the King of Detectives,
>   And when I am out on the trail
> All the animal criminals tremble,
>   And the criminal animals quail,
> For they know that I'll trace 'em
>   and chase 'em and place 'em
>   Behind the strong bars of the jail."

—but at that moment Freddy came to grief

FREDDY
THE DETECTIVE

by

WALTER R. BROOKS

with illustrations
by
KURT WIESE

ALFRED A. KNOPF · NEW YORK

THIS IS A BORZOI BOOK
PUBLISHED BY ALFRED A. KNOPF, INC.

Library of Congress Cataloging-in-Publication Data
Brooks, Walter R., 1886–1958. Freddy the detective. Summary: Freddy the pig does some detective work in order to solve the mystery of a missing toy train.
[1. Pigs—Fiction. 2. Animals—Fiction. 3. Mystery and detective stories] I. Wiese, Kurt, 1887— ill. II. Title. PZ7.B7994Frj 1987
[Fic] 86-40422
ISBN 0-394-88885-5 ISBN 0-394-98885-X (lib. bdg.)

Manufactured in the United States of America
2   4   6   8   10   9   7   5   3

INTRODUCTION

My best friend when I was growing up was Freddy the Pig, whose adventures Alfred A. Knopf has now republished. It took more than two dozen books to chronicle all of Freddy's adventures, for he was a prodigy: a pig of many parts. In these books, for example, you will meet him as politician, camper, pilot, balloonist, detective, poet, newspaper editor, and sportsman—uh, sports*pig*. Yet the one constant role he *never* failed to play was that of friend.

And it is the recurring theme of friendship warmly informing all of the Freddy books which elevates them to the status of American classics. When I was growing up, my friend Freddy taught me about the joys—and responsibilities—of friendship: of sharing and caring, of loyalty and constancy, of kindness, compassion, and forgiveness, and above all—of *helping*. Freddy's friends were often in danger; yet, even if Freddy was so frightened that his tail was completely uncurled, he gritted his teeth and did whatever was necessary to help. Growing up with the Freddy books, I learned a whole system of traditional values and enduring ethics.

Don't think for a minute that this means the books are preachy or moralistic or dull. On the contrary, they're exciting and unfailingly *funny*! The Freddy books are full of word play—of funny names and outrageous puns and amusing dialogue. Slapstick and satire are here, too, but the best of the books' humor arises out of the characters—out of Jinx the cat and Mrs. Wiggins the cow and Charles the rooster and others too numerous to mention, not only on the farm but also in Boomschmidt's Stupendous and Unexcelled Circus. Our friendship with these characters entitles us to laugh not *at* them but *with* them.

Finally, the Freddy books capture and preserve a uniquely American moment. Upstate New York is their setting, but they really belong to your hometown and mine, places that endure forever in our hearts.

You bet they're classics.

And my friend is a classic too. Welcome back, Freddy. You've been gone too long.

Michael Cart
City Librarian
Beverly Hills, California

FREDDY THE DETECTIVE

To

Elsie

CHAPTER I

FREDDY'S FIRST CASE

IT was hot. When Alice and Emma, the two white ducks, got tired of diving and swimming about in the pond, they climbed out on the bank and looked over toward the house where Mr. Bean, the farmer, lived, and: "Oh!" said Emma, "the house looks as if it was melting. All the straight lines—the roof and the door and the walls—are wiggling. Look, Alice."

"It always looks like that when it's hot," said Alice.

"Well, I don't like it," said Emma. "It makes me feel funny in my stomach. I think things ought to stay what they are, even if they *are* hot. Let's jump in again and cool off."

Alice looked at the water without much interest. It wasn't a very large pond, and in it were three cows and two horses and a dog and on the bank were half a dozen other animals who were resting after their dip. "Too much company," she said crossly, or as crossly as she could, for she was really a very mild duck. "I don't know why they call it a *duck*-pond. Just as soon as warm weather comes, every animal on the farm seems to think he has a perfect right to use it as a swimming-pool without so much as saying please. And just look at that, Emma!" she exclaimed. "What chance would you and I have in there now?"

Two of the cows, Mrs. Wiggins and Mrs. Wurzburger, were having a race across the pond and back. They splashed and floundered and snorted, making waves that would have upset the stoutest duck, while the ani-

4

mals on the bank cheered and shouted en-
couragement.

"Come on, let's take a walk," said Emma.
"Let's find a place in the shade where there's
a breeze. That water's just as hot as the air
is, anyway."

They waddled up the lane toward the
house, and in a corner of the fence they came
upon Jinx, the black cat, who was lying on
his back with all four paws in the air, trying
to keep cool.

"Hello, ducks!" he hailed them. "Gosh,
you look nice and cool!"

"Well, you don't," said Alice. "I should
think you'd stifle, lying in that breathless
corner. Why don't you come with us? We're
going to look for a breeze."

"Whoops!" shouted Jinx, jumping up
with a bound. "I'm with you, girls. Tell you
what: we'll go find Freddy. That pig'll be in
a cool spot, you bet. He knows how to be
comfortable better than any other animal
on this farm."

5

Freddy was indeed a very clever pig. It was he who had organized the animals on Mr. Bean's farm into a company, known as Barnyard Tours, Inc., which took parties of other animals on sightseeing trips. He knew how to read, and he had gathered together quite a library of the books and magazines and newspapers that different animals had brought in to pay for their trips with. He kept them in a corner of the pig-pen which he called his study.

The ducks knew that even if Freddy wasn't in a cool spot, he would have a new bit of interesting gossip, or some story he had just read, to tell them about, so they started out to find him.

"Have you heard about Everett's train of cars?" asked Jinx as they walked along.

"No," said the ducks. Everett and his sister, Ella, were the two adopted children of Mr. and Mrs. Bean, whom the animals had rescued the year before from a dreadful place where they had been living in the

6

North Woods. Because they had rescued them, the animals all felt a great interest in Ella and Everett, and they were fond of them too, so no two children ever had a better time. The ducks taught them to swim and the horses taught them to ride and the cat taught them how to climb and to move through the woods without making a sound, and Ferdinand, the crow, had even wanted to teach them how to fly, but of course that wasn't much use, because they didn't have any wings. But there were always animals to play games and do things with, and they certainly had as good a time as any children who ever lived.

"Well," said Jinx, "it's the funniest thing I ever heard of. When Everett went to sleep last night, the train was beside him on the bed. When he woke up this morning, it was gone. Mrs. Bean has looked all over the house, and I've done some looking on my own account. But it's gone; there's no doubt about that."

7

"Well, that *is* queer," said Emma. "You don't suppose he hid it himself, as a joke?"

"Oh no, not a chance. He's been looking everywhere all morning. He's very fond of that train. I'd like to get my claws on the one that took it!" the cat exclaimed fiercely.

"Mercy!" exclaimed Emma with a slight shudder. "I wish you wouldn't glare like that, Jinx. Alice and I didn't have anything to do with it."

"No, no; of course you didn't," replied the cat soothingly. "Imagine a duck being a burglar!" He laughed heartily.

But the ducks turned on him indignantly. "Well, I guess we could be burglars if we wanted to!" said Emma. "I guess we're not as poor-spirited as you seem to think!"

"I guess not, indeed!" put in Alice. "Look at our Uncle Wesley! I guess you know what he did, that time when that big old elephant escaped from the circus at Centerboro and tried to take a bath in our pond. He chased him off the place!"

8

"Oh sure!" said the cat. "Sure I remember." Jinx remembered how the elephant had laughed, too, when pompous little Uncle Wesley had ordered him out of the pond. But he didn't say anything to the ducks about that. "Well, anyway," he went on, "I think it's a shame, and we ought to do something about it.—Though it's too hot to do anything about anything today," he added, and stopped to wipe the perspiration from his whiskers with a fore-paw.

They walked round the house and down the road to the fence where the farm ended; then they walked back along the fence to the woods and across the back pasture, but saw no sign of Freddy.

"It's funny," said Jinx. "I felt sure we'd run into him. Let's sit down under this tree and rest awhile."

"You can if you want to," said Emma, "but I started out to find Freddy, and now I'm going to find him." Like all ducks, she was very stubborn, and when she had made

9

up her mind to anything, nothing could stop her.

"Oh, all right," said the cat good-naturedly. "Only it's so hot. Let's try the pig-pen. Maybe he's in his study."

But he wasn't in the pig-pen, and he wasn't in the stable or the cow-barn.

"He must be puttering round in the woods somewhere, then," said Alice. "Maybe he's calling on Peter." Peter was the bear whom the animals had brought back from the north the year before, and who now lived in a cave in Mr. Bean's woods.

"It'll be cooler in the woods, anyway," said Jinx. So they went back across the pasture and plunged into the green silence of the trees.

It was very still in the woods, and very dark after the glaring sunshine outside. They walked slowly along, calling: "Freddy! Hey, Freddy!" every now and then. Jinx liked the woods, but the ducks began to get a little nervous. "I don't like this," said Emma. "It's so dim and still, and I feel as if something were following us. There! Did you hear that?" She stopped, and they all looked back over their shoulders, for somewhere behind them a twig had snapped.

"Nonsense!" said Jinx. "There's nothing here to hurt you. Come along."

"Mmmmm," said Emma doubtfully, "I don't like noises behind me. Uncle Wesley always said: 'When you're out walking and hear noises behind you, it is better to go right home.'"

"But you're with *me*!" said Jinx.

"Oh, all right," said Emma. "We know

you won't let anything catch us"; and they went on.

But the ducks were very nervous, and they walked with their heads turned round so far backwards that they were continually tripping over roots and stones, and even Jinx began to feel a little uneasy, particularly as his ears, which were sharper than the ducks', told him that someone really was following them. He wasn't afraid for himself, for there was no animal in these woods that could hurt him, but he thought it might be a fox, and there's nothing a fox likes better for supper than a nice plump duck.

He was about to suggest that they turn back when Alice suddenly gave a terrified quack and tumbled over in a faint.

"Good gracious!" exclaimed Emma. "She must have seen something that frightened her terribly. She hasn't done that in I don't know when. No, no; there isn't anything you can do. She'll be all right in a minute. Just keep her head low. Dear me, I wish we were out of here!"

"We'll go right back," said Jinx, who was supporting the swooning duck in his paws. "There! She's coming round now. Well, Alice, you did give us a fright! What was it you saw?"

Alice's eyes opened slowly. "Where am I?" she murmured; then as she remembered, she scrambled to her feet. "There!" She pointed with her bill. "Right behind that clump of bushes. There was a face, with a long pointed white nose—" She broke off and shuddered violently. "It gave me such a turn!"

"You wait here," said Jinx. "I'll show him!" And he crouched low on the ground and crept noiselessly toward the bushes.

As he came close to them, the ducks saw him gather himself together, then spring clean over the bushes. There was a commotion among the leaves, a snarl, a shrill squeal of fright, and out into the open dashed

Freddy with Jinx on his back. The cat was cuffing the pig soundly about the head, but as they came near the ducks, he jumped down, and Freddy stopped, shook himself, and looked about him ruefully.

"You didn't have to be so rough, Jinx," he complained. "I wasn't doing any harm."

"You scared Alice, here, into a faint," said the cat angrily. "What on earth were you trying to do—play Indian?"

"I'm sorry, Alice," said Freddy. "I really didn't mean to scare you. I didn't think you saw me. I was just shadowing you."

"Shadowing!" said Jinx. "What's that?"

"Oh," said Freddy importantly, "it's a

term used by detectives. It means following you to see what you're up to. I'm going to be a detective, and I was practicing."

"Well, I don't know what a detective is," said Emma, "but you can just try it on somebody else next time. I think it's mean of you to scare us like that. You even scared Jinx."

"You did *not*!" said the cat quickly. "But you were trying to, and I'm going to get even with you for it, Freddy. I'm—"

"I wasn't; honestly I wasn't, Jinx," protested the pig. "Look here; I wasn't going to tell anybody about it, but I'll let you three in on it to make up for giving you such a scare. I got the idea from a book I found in the barn, *The Adventures of Sherlock Holmes*. It's the best book I've come across in a long time, and you'll admit I know something about literature. I'll venture to say that there isn't a pig in the country has a finer library or a wider knowledge of—"

"Oh, cut out the hot air," interrupted Jinx rudely, "and let's have the story."

"Well, it's this way," said Freddy. "This Sherlock Holmes was a great detective. Whenever a crime was committed, and nobody knew who committed it, they'd call in Sherlock Holmes, and he'd find the criminal."

"But how did he find him if nobody knew who he was?" asked Alice.

"Because he was so clever," Freddy replied. "Maybe the criminal would leave footprints behind, and then Holmes would find out who made them. Oh, he was a wonder! He saw little things about people that nobody else would notice, for one thing. He could look at you and tell about where you'd been and what you'd been doing, just by noticing these things. Why, I'll show you how it's done; it's easy when you know how. Look at Jinx, here. Look on his back. There are a lot of little pieces of grass and leaves in his fur. This is a piece of a leaf off a raspberry bush. The only raspberry bushes on the farm are around the fence up by the house, so we know he's been there. Then— how did they get on his back? Well, it's a hot day, and cats sometimes lie on their backs to get cool, so we can be pretty sure he has been sleeping on his back in the corner of the fence up by the house."

"Gosh, that's pretty good, Freddy," said Jinx.

"It really isn't so good," said Freddy modestly, "because I saw you sleeping there. But of course I could have told that you had been there anyway, as soon as I saw the leaves in your fur."

"But what were you following us for?" asked Alice.

"Why, just what I've been telling you. I was shadowing you. I was practicing being a detective. I followed you all around the farm. I didn't mean you to see me, of course. If I'd been a good detective, you wouldn't have known anything about it. I was trying to see what you were up to."

"Why didn't you ask, then?" said Emma.

"Detectives don't *ask*!" said Freddy impatiently. "*Can't* you understand?"

"No, I can't. You were taking such a lot of bother to find out something we'd have told you right off. We were just looking for you!"

"He means that he was pretending that we were criminals," Jinx explained. "Of course if we had been, and we'd been going to steal something, we wouldn't have told him. It wouldn't be any use to ask then. See?"

"Oh," said Emma, and Alice said: "Oh," in just the same tone. And then they both said in their little flat voices: "Let's go back."

Jinx winked at Freddy. They were very fond of the ducks. Alice and Emma were the kindest-hearted little creatures in the world, but it was useless to try to explain

18

anything to them that they didn't already know about, and even with things they knew about they sometimes got terribly mixed up.

They waddled along happily together, their fright entirely forgotten, and Jinx and Freddy followed them, talking about detectives. Freddy told one or two of Sherlock

Holmes's adventures out of the book, and Jinx was greatly interested. By and by he said: "Look here, Freddy, I forgot all about it in the excitement, but there's a job for a detective on this farm now." And he told about the missing train.

Freddy was all enthusiasm. "I'll get on the job right away," he said. "I'll find that train, you bet! There are a lot of mysteries on a farm like this and I'll solve 'em all. Maybe I can write them up in a book: 'The Adventures of Freddy the Detective.' And this'll be the first one. Freddy's First Case."

"If you find the train," said Jinx.

"Oh dear," said Freddy mournfully, "I like you, Jinx, but why do you always have to say things like that? Of course I'll find it."

"Sure you will, old pig," said the cat with a grin. "Because *I'm* going to help you."

CHAPTER II

THE RATS DEFY THE LAW

"THE first thing to do," said Freddy, "is to Visit the Scene of the Crime."

The smaller animals always helped Mrs. Bean with the housework, and were in and out of the house a good deal all day, so when Jinx and Freddy went in the kitchen door and up the back stairs, Mrs. Bean merely glanced up from the peas that two rabbits were helping her shell and said: "Be careful of those stairs, animals. They're pretty steep. I don't want you should hurt yourselves."

The children's room was the front bedroom over the porch, next to Mr. and Mrs.

Bean's. Jinx started to walk across the floor, but Freddy stopped him. "Please don't disturb anything," he said, "until I have finished my investigation."

"Oh, I'm not disturbing anything. What's the matter with you?" demanded the cat.

"You're disturbing the clues," replied the pig testily. "All crimes have clues, and if you follow the clues, you find the criminal."

"If I knew what clues were, I'd know better what you were talking about," said Jinx.

But Freddy did not answer. He was being a detective for all he was worth. He went very carefully over the floor, and then he examined the bed and the window-sill, and finally he got a tape-measure out of Ella's little sewing-basket and measured the height of the sill and the distance from the bed to the window and several other things. Jinx sat down by the door and watched, trying hard to look superior and sarcastic. But it's hard to look superior and sarcastic all by yourself when nobody's paying any atten-

tion to you, so after a while he gave it up and
went to sleep.

A little later he woke up again. Freddy
was standing looking out of the window,
wrapped in thought. "Well," said Jinx,
"found any of those—what do you call 'em?
—clues you were looking for?"

"I have," said Freddy importantly.
"What's more, I know who stole the train."

The cat jumped up. "Gosh, Freddy, do
you really? Who was it?"

"I'll tell you in a minute. Let me ask you
a few questions, first. I want to get my case
complete. Now, was this window open last
night?"

"I suppose so," replied Jinx. "They all
sleep with their windows open. Mighty unhealthy habit, I call it, but—"

"And the door was shut, I suppose," interrupted Freddy.

"Sure. I was around the house on and off
all night. I know it was shut."

"Did you hear any noises last night?"

23

"That's a foolish question," said the cat. "I always hear noises, every night. There are some noises that go on all night, like the clock ticking and Mr. Bean snoring, and then I heard the wind going around the house, and the furniture creaking, and—"

"No, no," interrupted Freddy impatiently, "I mean unusual noises. Think carefully now."

"H'm," said Jinx thoughtfully, "why, let's see. I heard one thing I don't usually hear. Those four flies that sleep on the kitchen ceiling—I caught one of them this morning, by the way—they woke up and got quarreling about something in the night. Of course that's not exactly what you'd call a noise; even I could hardly hear it. And then, there *was* something, it seems to me. What was it? I just faintly remember— Oh, I know! It was a couple of thumps."

"Thumps?"

"Yes. Outside somewhere."

"What kind of thumps?"

24

"Oh, I don't know. Just thumps. I thought maybe it was some of those coons from over in the woods. They're always playing monkey-shines at night. But I was too sleepy to go look."

"Ah," said Freddy, "I thought so. Well, my case is complete without that, but it all

hangs together very nicely. A very nice piece of detective work. See here, Jinx. I'll show you just how I solved the case. Here's the first clue I discovered. We'll call it Exhibit A. What do you make of that?"

There were some scratches on the white paint of the window-sill, and in several of them were traces of green paint. Jinx looked at them, sniffed of them, and said: "Ah! Just so!" because he couldn't think of anything else to say.

"That doesn't mean anything to you?" asked Freddy.

"Yes, yes. Quite!" said Jinx hastily. "Green paint. Very significant."

"I'm glad you follow me," said Freddy. "Now for Exhibit B." And he took Jinx over to the bed and showed him half a dozen very fine, very short dark gray hairs on the pillow.

Jinx looked at the hairs, but when he sniffed at them, he sniffed so hard that he blew them on to the floor.

"Hey!" shouted Freddy. "Be a little careful, can't you? You're destroying the evidence! We need those for our case."

"Case of what—measles?" said the cat contemptuously. "Say, look here, Freddy; are you trying to kid me, or are you just plain silly? You talk about those little old gray hairs and that green paint as if you'd

26

found a pitcher of cream. If this is all there is to your detective business, I'm going. I know lots of better ways of having fun than—"

"Oh, wait a minute!" exclaimed the pig. "Gosh, Jinx, I thought you *understood* what it meant. You *said* you did. Look here. Those cars in the train are painted green, aren't they? Well, what does that paint mean, then? It means that the cars rubbed on the window-sill when the thief was taking them out of the window last night, doesn't it?"

"H'm. I see what you're getting at," said Jinx.

"All right," went on Freddy. "Now, what kind of hairs were those I showed you?"

"Those hairs? I don't know. Just hairs."

"Oh, use a little sense! Were they Ella's? Or Mrs. Bean's?"

"No, of course not. Hairs like that—why, I suppose they might be cat hairs."

"Where is there a gray cat in this neighborhood?" asked Freddy.

"H'm. Mice, then," said Jinx. "No," he added, "they're too coarse for mouse hairs. But—rats!" he exclaimed suddenly. "By George, they're rat hairs, Freddy! Well, of all the nerve!"

Jinx was really very much upset, for the presence of a rat in the house was against all the rules. When Jinx had first come to the farm, several years earlier, there had been a family of rats living in the house, and several of them in the barn. When Jinx had ordered them out, they had just laughed at him, but Jinx was a brave and stalwart cat and a fierce fighter, and after several battles in which the rats had got much the worst of it, they had met him one night under a flag of truce and had agreed that if he would let them alone, they would all move down into the woods and would not enter either house or barn again. Until now they had kept the agreement.

"I can't believe it," said Jinx. "Those are rat hairs, all right, but there's only one way a rat could get into this room. He couldn't climb up the porch. He'd have to come in the door. And the door was shut all night. I don't believe any rat would dare come in during the day-time and hide."

"He wouldn't have to," said Freddy. "Look under the bed, Jinx."

The cat went under the bed and came out in a moment looking more worried than ever. "A fresh rat-hole!" he exclaimed. "Yes, there's no doubt about it. But it must have been a job to get that train of cars out of the window. I suppose they pushed them out and then got out on the porch roof and pushed them over the edge."

"And those were the thumps you heard," said Freddy. "Now come outside. They couldn't have carried the cars off. Each car is as big as a rat, as there were four of them and a tender, all fastened together. They must have dragged them, and we can probably find where they dragged them to."

In the big flower-bed in front of the porch six or seven squirrels were hard at work, pulling out weeds and raking with their claws and then sweeping the dirt smooth with their tails.

"Hey, Bill," called Freddy to the largest squirrel, who seemed to be the foreman, "come here a minute. I want to ask you something."

Bill dusted off his paws, growled to the other workmen to "keep busy, now, and no loafing while my back's turned," and came over to the pig.

"I suppose, Bill, you've heard about this train of cars that's missing, haven't you?" asked Freddy.

"Couldn't very well help it, sir," said the squirrel. "Everybody's talking about it."

"Well," said the pig, "we have reason to believe that the thief took it out of the window and pushed it off the roof. Now, I wonder if when you started work here this morning, you noticed any traces of where it fell into the flower-bed?"

"That I did, sir," replied the foreman. "That's what it must have been, though I didn't think of it at the time. A leaf was broken off one of those big cannas, and there was a big dent in the dirt, just where —" He broke off to shout angrily at one of the workmen. "Hey, Caspar! Don't pull that up! It's not a weed! Can't I ever teach you fellows the difference between chick-weed and nasturtiums? You've got no more brains than a chipmunk!—Excuse me, sir," he apologized to Freddy. "You can't trust these fellows a minute. They know the difference all right, but they pretend they think the nasturtiums are weeds so they can pull 'em up and eat 'em. They like the taste."

"Quite so, quite so," said Freddy hastily. "But you were saying—?"

"Dear, dear, what was I saying?" The squirrel scratched his ear thoughtfully.

31

"Oh, yes—right to the left, there, was where the dent was. And I remember that you could see where something had been dragged off in the direction of the barn. You can't see it now, since the dew has dried off the grass, but 'twas plain as plain. Straight down toward the barn, sir."

Freddy thanked the squirrel, and he and

Jinx went to the barn, to see Hank, the old white horse.

"Ah, Freddy," said Hank, "we don't see you round here nowadays as much as we might. But I suppose you're busy with your books, reading and writing poetry."

"Oh, poetry's all right," said Freddy, "but I've got something really important to do now. I'm a detective."

"Think of that!" said Hank admiringly. "And what do you—er, well—what are you detecting today?"

"I'm on the trail of a gang of thieves," replied the pig. "They stole Everett's train of cars last night, and I believe they've brought it down here. At least, they came by here with it, and I wondered if you heard or saw anything of them."

Hank chewed thoughtfully on a mouthful of hay. "No," he said. "I don't recollect anything. Who stole it?"

Freddy said they had reason to believe it was rats.

"Rats in the house!" exclaimed Hank. "Why, that's bad for you, Jinx. What'll Mr. Bean say when he finds out?"

"I guess it *is* bad for me!" said the cat. "Darn those rats anyway! I never yet knew a rat who could keep his word! Now I'll have to begin all over again."

"Now you speak of it," said Hank thoughtfully, "I remember that I've been

hearing some funny noises lately. Little rustlings and squeakings under the floor. I
never thought of rats, because they'd promised not to come in here, but I ain't so sure
now. Maybe they've moved back into their
old quarters, where they used to live before
you came."

This piece of news upset Jinx even more,
for the rats had had a large establishment
under the barn, a maze of tunnels and pas-
sages and underground rooms. He jumped
down from the manger where he had been
sitting, and went outside, followed by
Freddy. "Their main entrance used to be
under the foundations at the back," he said.
"We'll see if it shows any signs of having
been used lately."

But just as they came out the door a gray
shape darted across an open space and into
the shelter of a clump of weeds that grew
close to the barn wall.

Jinx leaped after it. "Hey, you!" he
shouted angrily. "Come out of there!" But

the rat had dived down a hole and disappeared.

Jinx turned to Freddy, trembling with rage. "Can you beat it?" he demanded. "They're here all right. That was old Simon. He was their leader in all the fights I had with them. The sly old wretch! I wonder what they're up to. They wouldn't dare come back if they didn't have some pretty good scheme in their heads."

"Let's have a talk with them," suggested Freddy. "Send one of the mice down with a flag of truce. Maybe we can find out something."

So Eeny, one of the mice who lived in the barn, was sent down with a flag of truce, and pretty soon up came old Simon with two of his sons, Zeke and Ezra.

"Hello, Jinx," said Simon with an oily smile. "Long time since I've had the pleasure of seeing you. You're looking well, remarkably well for a cat. Though a little worried. Something on your mind?"

"Come, cut out the soft soap!" said Jinx roughly. "Look here, Simon; what's the big idea? I want to know what you're doing in this barn."

Simon looked surprised. "Why, Jinx—it's our old home. Our old family mansion. Why shouldn't we be here?"

"You know blame well," said Jinx angrily. "You agreed two years ago—"

"Oh yes, that agreement." Simon waved a paw airily. "You didn't really take that seriously, did you? It seemed the best way, at the time, to settle our little misunderstanding. But of course this is our home; you couldn't expect us to go live down in those damp, musty woods forever. Could you, now?"

"You certainly won't live forever if you come back to the barn," said Jinx dryly.

"Ha, ha!" laughed Simon; and his two sons laughed "Ha, ha, ha!" and smoothed their whiskers with their paws. "You will have your joke, Jinx.—But come, let's be serious. It seems to us that every animal has a right to live where he wants to. We've talked it all over. All you other animals—cows and pigs and dogs and horses—have warm comfortable houses to live in. Why should the rats be the only ones to live in gloomy, unhealthy burrows in the ground?"

"Because you're thieves, that's why!" exclaimed Jinx. "I wouldn't have any objection to your living in the barn, and neither would Mr. Bean, but you steal the grain and everything else you can lay your paws on, and you gnaw holes in everything and destroy property. That's why."

The old gray rat spread out his paws.

"But we have to live! Even the humble rats have to live."

Jinx laughed a harsh laugh. "Oh, no, you don't!" he said. "Not while I've got my claws and teeth. Well," he added, "I see you've made up your minds, so I suppose it's war again, eh?"

But Simon did not seem disturbed. "War?" he said. "Why war? There won't be any war. We don't have to fight you, Jinx, to live in the barn." He grinned wickedly. "You may think we do, but we don't. Things have changed, Jinx."

"Is that so?" said the cat. "Well, I don't know what you're up to, but take my word for it, it won't last long. I give you warning —the next time I see a rat in the barn, it's good-bye, rat. And that means you, and you, and you," and he glared at each of them in turn so fiercely that they moved away a little uncomfortably.

"Well," said Simon, "if that's all you got

38

us up here for, we might as well be going, pleasant as it is to see you again. Boys—"

"Wait a minute," interrupted Freddy. "Simon, what about the train of toy cars you stole last night?"

Zeke and Ezra looked startled, but Simon merely grinned. "So—o—o!" he said slowly, "you found out about that, did you?" There was a faint gleam of admiration in his beady black eyes. "Very clever of you, Freddy. Not that it will be any advantage to you. You'd have found out we had it soon enough."

"We expect you to give it back," said the pig. "Every animal on the farm will be sore at you if you don't. They're all very fond of Everett, and—"

"Oh, sure; they're all fond of Everett!" interrupted Zeke angrily. "He pets 'em and feeds 'em. But what has he ever done for us? And what has Mr. Bean ever done for us? Set traps and mixed poison—that's what he's done for us! Driven us out of our comfortable homes! And you think we should be

39

nice and kind and do things for him and say 'pretty please' just because he's a man and owns this farm. Well, we're sick of men. Men are all alike, selfish know-it-alls, and if you don't do as they say—out you go! But you just wait! You and the rest of the stuck-up animals on this farm that think you're so smart! We've got a few tricks up our sleeve yet. You wait till you see that train of cars the next time; you'll laugh out of the other side of your mouths! Just wait till—"

But here Simon interrupted him. "Come, come, son; there's nothing to be gained by violence. You must excuse him, gentlemen. My son is so impetuous. Dear, dear! I suppose we were all that way once. Ah, youth, youth! Even you were once young, I suppose, Freddy, though now you've become so stupid and fat and stodgy that no doubt you've forgotten those far-off days when you were a gay squealing piglet, and the whole world was your trough."

"I'm not old and I'm not stodgy," snapped

Freddy; but Jinx said: "You're impudent, Simon. And no rat is ever impudent to me twice. I'll give you till tonight to clear out of the barn and to return that train. If by eight o'clock it's not done, then it's war! And understand me: when I say war, I mean *war*! Now, git!" And he bared his teeth in such a ferocious grin that the three rats, with a snarl, dived down the hole and disappeared.

"You know," said Freddy, as they walked back to the house, "there's really something in what they say. It must be rather hard to be driven out of your home and hunted from pillar to post."

"You have a sympathetic nature, Freddy," replied his friend. "It does you credit, but your sympathy is wasted on these rats. Nobody'd hunt 'em if they'd behave themselves. And, anyway, if all animals behaved themselves, how could you go on being a detective? There wouldn't be any crimes for you to detect."

"I suppose that's so," sighed the pig. "Perhaps I shouldn't be a detective after all, Jinx. I shall always feel so sorry for the criminals when I find them that I'll probably let them go."

"Huh, that's silly!" said the cat. "I feel sorry for those rats—*yes*, I do! But what'll you bet they bring back the train and leave the barn tonight?"

"I bet they don't," replied Freddy promptly. "They've got something up their sleeve, all right. Did you see how Simon stopped Zeke when he was afraid he'd say too much? No, sir! They're going to start something, and they're going to start it right away or I miss my guess. You're going to watch the barn tonight, I suppose?"

"Sure, I'll have to."

"Well, I'm going to watch with you, then," said Freddy. "You see, a detective's job isn't finished when he's found out who the criminal is. He has to put him in jail.

42

I'm going home now to think this case over. Meet you in Hank's stall at eight o'clock." And he trotted off, stopping now and then to peer intently at the ground as if searching for further clues.

CHAPTER III

THE ARMORED TRAIN

THUNDER rumbled distantly, and the orchard trees stood out black against the flickering western sky as Freddy stole into the barn and made his way silently to Hank's stall.

"Hello," whispered Hank. "Jinx has gone up to take a turn around the hay-mow. We'll be getting some rain presently, I expect. I guess Mr. Bean will be glad; everything's got pretty well burned up this long dry spell. But I've known for two days we'd get a storm. I always feel it in that off hind leg of mine. Stiffened up something dreadful today."

"Sh-h-h!" hissed Freddy. "Mustn't talk. Rats'll hear."

Hank grunted something under his breath and then was silent. Freddy could hear the crisp dry swish as hay was pulled from the rack, and the slow comfortable munching that followed. The flicker of lightning was almost continuous now in the square of the open doorway, and the approaching drums of the thunder shook the windless air. Then something furry brushed against Freddy's shoulder and he jumped violently and let out a startled squeal.

"Shut up, you idiot," came Jinx's whisper. "It's only me."

Freddy was so ashamed that he couldn't think of anything to say. What would Sherlock Holmes think of a detective who jumped almost out of his skin when his friend touched him?

"I thought I heard some gnawing going on," murmured Jinx, "but I can't find anything. We'll just wait awhile."

Freddy wondered what good he would be if they did find the rats in the hay-mow. Pigs are stout fighters, but they like to fight in the open; and up there in the pitch-dark, floundering about in the hay—well, the idea didn't appeal to him much. Then he reflected that after all both he and Jinx wanted first of all to find out just what the rats were up to and where they had hidden the train

of cars. There probably wouldn't be any fighting tonight.

The storm came nearer. A puff of cool air came through the doorway and blew chaff in Freddy's eyes. Between the thunder claps he could hear the *thump* of windows being put down in the house. And then with a sharp rattle, and then with a roar that was louder than the thunder, the rain came down upon the barn.

Jinx put his mouth close to Freddy's ear. "They can't hear us now," he shouted. "Let's get upstairs. I have an idea that if anything happens, it will be up there, because that's where the big feed-box is. They'll go after those oats, and then—Wham-o!" And the cat gave his friend a joyous whack on the back.

As they reached the top of the stairs, the rain stopped suddenly. There was a moment of silence, and through it the friends heard a queer rattling noise, as if someone was dragging empty tin cans across the floor. A distant flicker of lightning lit the loft dimly, and Freddy saw something that made queer prickles travel up his spine. A long low shape was moving slowly across from the hay-mow toward the feed-box.

If it was an animal, it was the strangest animal Freddy had ever seen. It was nearly four feet long, but not more than four or

48

five inches high. It seemed to glide along like a snake, and as it moved it rattled and squeaked, as if its insides were full of machinery.

"I'm going," said Freddy firmly, but as he backed toward the stairs, there came a sharper flash of lightning, and he saw what the strange animal was. It was the train of cars.

A train of toy cars that moves all by itself in an empty loft during a thunder-storm would make even a policeman a little uneasy. But though Freddy was scared, like all true detectives he was more curious than frightened, and he stood his ground. For a minute it was dark and they could hear nothing through the crashing thunder. Then came another flash, and as the train of cars was swallowed up again in the darkness, Jinx sprang.

Freddy waited. As the thunder died away again, he heard a rattling and banging in the middle of the floor, and then the loft seemed to be full of the squeaking laughter of rats. "He-he-he!" they giggled. "Smarty-cat Jinx! He can't catch us now!" Lightning danced over the landscape outside, and for what seemed quite a long time Freddy watched a strange battle between the cat and

the train. Jinx leaped upon it, bit it, pounded and slashed at it with his paws, tried to knock it over; and all the time it moved jerkily on toward the feed-box, accompanied by the shouts and jeers of rats. Then as darkness poured into the barn again, Jinx gave up and bounded back to Freddy's side. "Back downstairs," he panted. "It's no use. We'll have to try something else."

Back in Hank's stall again, Jinx stretched out on the floor to rest, and Freddy said: "I'd have tried to help you, Jinx, but I didn't understand what it was all about or what you were trying to do. And, frankly, that train of cars, moving all by itself, had me scared."

"It had me scared at first, too," admitted Jinx. "But my eyes are pretty good in the dark, you know, and I saw what was inside the cars."

"Inside them! You mean—" A light suddenly burst on Freddy. "The rats!" He saw it all. Those four cars had wheels, but there were no floors in them, and each was big enough to hold a good-sized rat. Easy enough for the rat to get in, and then he was as safe as a turtle inside his shell.

"Of course," said Jinx. "And you see what it means. They can get from their holes to the feed-box and back, and I can't stop 'em. Of course if Mr. Bean sweeps up all the grain that's around on the floor, and stops up that hole in the side of the box, it will be

harder for them. Then they'll have to get out
of their armored train. But I don't want Mr.
Bean to find out about it. He won't know
anything about the train, you see, and he'll
just think I'm no good at my job."

"But what can we do?" asked Freddy.

"Well, you're the detective, aren't you?"
asked Jinx irritably. "You've done a lot of
big talk about how you were in charge of
the case, and so on. Oh, I admit you did a
good job finding out who stole the train—
you mustn't think I'm cross at you. I'm just
sore about the whole business. But if you're
going in for being a detective, this is your
chance to get a reputation. You've got as
much at stake as I have."

Freddy didn't sleep much that night. He
knew what Jinx had said was so. Sherlock
Holmes would have rounded up those rats
and had them behind the bars in a couple of
days. But he couldn't think of anything to
do. He was up early the next morning, reading the stories in the Sherlock Holmes book,

but the cases were all so different from his that he found nothing to help him. He went down to the barn.

"They're up there," said Hank. "Hard at it since before daylight." And indeed from where he was, Freddy could hear the rattle of the train being drawn across the floor by its crew of rats. He climbed the stairs cautiously. There it was, moving away from the feed-box. He could see the rats' feet moving as they pushed it along, and the tender was piled full of yellow oats.

"There's *one* thing I can do," said Freddy to himself, and he made a dash for the train, knocked over the tender, and spilled the grain out on the floor. But the rats only laughed. "Pooh, pooh for Freddy!" they shouted derisively. "We'll get more than that the next trip. Do you want to know how we work it, silly pig? Four of us go over and eat all we can hold. The next trip, four others go and eat all they can hold. Then, the next trip, four others go and—"

53

But Freddy was tearing mad. To be mocked at by rats is more than any self-respecting pig can stand. He jumped at the train and tried to get his snout under it and fling it in the air, but it was too low. He did manage, however, to push two cars over on

their sides, and while the rats lay there kicking, he tried to bite them. But he only succeeded in breaking one of his front teeth on a car wheel, and before he gave up, one of the rats had nipped him sharply in the ear. Then he went back downstairs, followed by more uncomplimentary remarks than he had ever heard before at one time in his life.

Freddy felt pretty low.

CHAPTER IV

THE MYSTERY OF EGBERT

FREDDY'S failure bothered him a good deal. The rats soon spread the news of it far and wide, and Freddy couldn't go outside the pig-pen without meeting animals who asked him how the case was getting on and whether he had got the train of cars back yet. "They're all very kind and sympathetic," he said to Jinx, "because nobody likes Simon and his family. But I won't get any other cases if I don't solve this one pretty quick. And from the way it looks now, it's going to take some time."

"Yes, and I'll be out of a job if Mr. Bean finds out," replied the cat. "We've got to do something, and do it now. I suppose you've heard the song the rats are singing about you?"

Freddy grunted angrily. Yes, he had heard it all right. Every time he went near the barn, the rats began shouting it out at the top of their lungs, and they used it as a sort of marching song when they trundled the train back and forth between their hole and the feed-box.

Freddy, the sleuth,
He busted a tooth,
He's a silly old bonehead, and that is the truth.

Freddy the pig,
He talks very big,
But all that he's good for's to guzzle and swig.

Freddy the fat,
He's never learned that
It takes forty-nine pigs to equal one rat.

And there were many more verses. It was not very good, just as a song, but it irritated

Freddy frightfully, and that was what the rats wanted. It would irritate anyone to have a song like that yelled at him morning, noon, and night.

"Well," said Jinx, "I'm counting on you. There's nothing much I can do but hang round the barn and try to get a crack at Simon when he's not inside that train. Haven't you got any ideas at all?"

"Sure, I've got ideas," Freddy replied. "I'm working on the thing all the time. But you know how detectives work. They wouldn't be any good if they told everything they were doing. Everything is going satisfactorily, though a little slower than I had hoped. But I'm making as good progress as could be expected."

"Humph!" said the cat. "As good progress as I could expect from you—and that's just none at all." But he said it under his breath, for perhaps Freddy *did* have an idea —he was really a very clever pig—and it was no good offending him. Jinx needed his help too badly for that.

But Freddy really had no ideas at all. There was no good using force; he had tried that, and all he had got out of it was a broken tooth that sent his family into fits of laughter whenever he smiled. Anyway, detectives seldom used force; they used guile. He went back to his library and got comfortable and tried to think up some guile to use on the rats. And as usual when he lay perfectly still and concentrated for a short time, he fell asleep.

He was awakened by a timid but persistent tapping at the door. "Come in," he said sleepily, and then as a white nose and two white ears appeared round the edge of the door, he jumped up. "Ah, Mrs. Winnick," he said as the rest of an elderly rabbit followed the ears into the room; "long time since I have seen you. What can I do for you today?"

Mrs. Winnick was a widow who lived

down by the edge of the woods. In her day she had been as pretty a young rabbit as you could wish to see, but since the loss of her husband the cares of providing for a large family had taken every bit of her time and energy. She took no part in the gay social life of the other animals in the neighbor-

hood, and they seldom saw her, though they were good to her, and one or other of them was always taking a fresh head of lettuce or a couple of carrots down to her, for they suspected that she and the children did not always get enough food.

"Oh, Mr. Freddy," she burst out, "it's about Egbert. He's disappeared, and whatever I shall do I don't know. He was always such a good boy, too—kind and helpful, and willing to look after the baby. With the other children it's play, play, play all day long, but Egbert—" And she began to cry.

Freddy was not greatly disturbed by her tears. Most animals don't like to cry because it makes their eyes red, but white rabbits have red eyes anyway, so crying doesn't make them look any different. And as they are very sentimental and tender-hearted little animals, and easily upset, they cry a good deal.

"Come, come," said Freddy briskly. "Just tell me all about it, and we'll see what can be done. I'm sure it's not as bad as you think. Now, do you want me to help you find Egbert?" And as she nodded tearful assent, "Well," he continued, "let's get at the facts. Let's see—Egbert. He's your eighth oldest, isn't he? Or ninth?"

"Twelfth," she replied, "and always such a good—"

"Yes," said Freddy quickly. "And when did you last see him?"

After asking a good many questions Freddy got Mrs. Winnick's story. The night before Egbert had taken several of the children up through the woods to Jones's Creek to get some watercress. At nine o'clock the children had come home without him. They had not found any good watercress, and Egbert had said that he would go farther down the creek to a place he knew where there was sure to be some, but that they must go home, as it was their bedtime, and their mother would worry. Mrs. Winnick had put the children to bed and had presently gone to bed herself. But this morning Egbert's bed was empty. He had not come home, and nothing had been seen or heard of him since.

Freddy consoled the weeping widow as best he could. "I'll get to work on it right away," he said, "and meanwhile don't worry. I'll soon have Egbert back for you. By the way, who sent you to me?"

"It was the children," said the rabbit. "They'd heard about your setting up to be a detective, and they wanted me to come and see you. Not that I have any faith in it—excuse me, sir. But you haven't been at it very long, have you?"

"No," Freddy admitted, "but there always has to be a first time, doesn't there? Even Sherlock Holmes made a start once, didn't he? Don't you worry, ma'am. I've made a deep study of the subject, and there isn't an animal in the country that knows more about detecting than I do. Why, I've read a whole book about it."

Mrs. Winnick seemed satisfied with this and went off home, stopping after every three or four hops to cry a little and blow her nose. Freddy wasted no time, but set out at once for the creek. He found the water-cress bed which Egbert had visited with his little brothers and sisters, then went slowly on downstream, keeping a sharp look-out for any signs of the missing rabbit. Once he saw where some wintergreen leaves had been nibbled, and once, in a sandy place, he saw the plain imprint of a rabbit's foot, so he knew he was on the right track. And then where the stream widened out, just before it took a bend round to the right to join the river, he found another big bed of cress, and in the swampy shore a large number of rabbit's footprints.

Freddy had been very happy when he started out. Although he had failed to get back Everett's train of cars, Mrs. Winnick's visit had cheered him up a lot. Here was a new problem. He would solve it and prove to his friends that he was a real detective after all. But now this problem was just as bad as the other one. What was he going to do? These were Egbert's footprints all right, but what good did they do him? There ought to be some clue that he could follow up. There always was in the Sherlock Holmes stories. "You can't solve a case without clues," he muttered unhappily. "These might be clues to Sherlock Holmes, but to me they're just a lot of footprints." And he sat down on the bank to think.

He was thinking so hard that for some time he did not see a small rabbit who hopped down out of the woods to the cress bed, picked a few stalks, then hopped back up among the trees. The rabbit had made several trips before Freddy suddenly caught sight of him.

The rabbit hadn't seen Freddy either, and when the pig started up suddenly, he dodged quickly behind a bush.

"So *you're* the one who made all those footprints in the mud here, are you?" said Freddy.

"Yes, sir," came a small anxious voice from behind the bush. "Isn't it all right, sir?"

"Sure it's all right," said the pig. "Come out; I won't hurt you. I'm looking for a rabbit about your size. Haven't seen one around, have you?"

The rabbit hopped timidly out. "No, sir," he said. "Who was he, sir?"

"Ah," said Freddy mysteriously, "*I'm* the one to be asking the questions. I'm a detective. Just you answer up briskly, young fellow. Haven't seen any other rabbits around, eh?"

"No, sir—"

"No other footprints in the mud when you came here?"

"I don't think so, sir. You see, I—"

"How long have you been here?"

"Since last night, sir. You see, I came to get some watercress, and as I was—"

Freddy stopped him. "That's enough," he said severely. "Please just answer the questions I ask you, without adding anything of your own. Just answer yes or no. You heard no unusual noises?"

"Yes, sir—I mean no, sir," said the rabbit, who was getting confused.

"What do you mean—'yes, sir, no, sir'?" said Freddy. "Please give me a straight answer. Did you or did you not hear any unusual noises?"

"No, sir—I mean—" The rabbit gulped. "—no, sir."

"Good," said the pig. "That's the stuff; a straight answer to a straight question. And —ha, h'm—let me see—" He hadn't found out anything, and yet he couldn't think of any more questions to ask. "Well, ah—what are you doing here anyway?"

But the rabbit didn't answer. "Come, come," said Freddy sharply. "Answer me! What are you—"

66

But the rabbit interrupted him by bursting into tears. "You told me to answer yes or no," he sobbed, "and you can't answer that question yes or no. I c-came here to get watercress, an' I was just going home an' I found a little bird with a hurt wing, and I thought I ought to stay with it, an' I know my mother'll worry, b-but I don't like to leave the bird all alone, an' now you come an' ask me a lot of questions I don't know the answers to, an'—" Here he broke down entirely and cried so hard that he got the hiccups.

Freddy was a kind-hearted animal, but he had been so absorbed in asking questions in a thoroughly detective-like manner that he hadn't really noticed that he was frightening the rabbit so badly that the poor little creature couldn't give him any information even if he had it to give. In this Freddy was more like a real detective than he realized. Some detectives will ask a simple question like "What is your name?" in so frightening a

voice that the person he asks can't even remember whether he has a name or not.

"There, there," said Freddy, patting the
rabbit on the back, "I'm sorry I scared you.
It's all right. Where is this bird?"

"Up in a hollow behind that tree," hiccuped the little animal.

"All right," said Freddy. "I'll look after
him for you. You run along home. I've got
to find this other rabbit I was telling you
about, but first I'll see that the bird is taken
care of. Run along and tell your mother not
to worry any more."

The rabbit wasted no time, but trotted off,
still crying, and hiccuping occasionally
through his tears, and Freddy went in search
of the bird. He found it presently—a fledgling wood thrush, too young to talk yet. Beside it was a small heap of watercress which
the rabbit had evidently been trying to
feed it.

"Tut, tut," said Freddy. "Feeding an in-
fant like that watercress! He'll be sick. And

he's hidden here so that his mother couldn't possibly find him. That rabbit has a kind heart, but he certainly isn't very bright." He picked up the little thrush carefully in his mouth and carried it, fluttering feebly, out into an open space, then went back into the bushes and sat down. In five minutes there was a rush of wings and the mother thrush alighted beside the hungry fledgling and began consoling him with little chirps. Freddy slipped away without waiting to be thanked.

"Now," he said to himself, "for Egbert. Though how in the world I'm to find him I don't know. But I've *got* to or I'll never dare to show my face in the farm-yard again. I wish I'd never tried to be a detective, that's what I wish!"

On a chance he decided to go a little farther down the creek, at least as far as the hermit's house, a deserted cabin which stood on the other side of the stream. Perhaps some of the waterside animals might have seen the missing rabbit.

But he had not gone far before something drove all thought of Egbert from his mind. There were sounds coming from the hermit's house. Shouts and rough laughter and occasional pistol-shots. What a chance for a detective! Freddy crept forward; then, finding that the bushes on the opposite bank were too high to permit him to see what was going on, he plunged into the water, swam quietly across, and worked his way up toward the house. And this is what he saw:

Hanging from the limb of a tall tree in front of the house was a swing made of two ropes and a board for a seat. A big man with a cap pulled down over his eyes, and his coat collar turned up, was swinging in long, dizzy swoops. He had a revolver in his hand, and at the top of his swing, when he was level with the top of the house, he would shoot the revolver and try to hit the chimney. A smaller man was sitting in a rocking-chair on the porch. He wore a black mask over his face, and no cap, and was knitting busily away at a woolen muffler.

Pretty soon the big man stopped swinging. "Come now, Looey," he shouted. "It's your turn now."

The small man shook his head. "No, Red, I must get this muffler done. We'll both want to wrap up warm tomorrow night; we'll be out late."

"Oh, come on," said Red. "Take a couple of shots anyway. Bet you can't beat me. I got two out of seven."

The other got up rather unwillingly. "Well, all right. But you have got to promise

71

to be more careful. I worry about you all the time. You remember that last bank we robbed; it was a rainy night and you didn't wear your rubbers, and you caught a bad cold."

"Yes, yes, Looey," Red replied. "I'll be careful. Come on, now. Into the swing."

"You'll have to push me, Red," said Looey, taking a large revolver from the pocket of his coat. He seated himself in the swing, and the big man started him swinging. Higher and higher he went, until at each push Red was running right under him. Then when he was high enough, he aimed the revolver, and bang! a brick flew from the chimney.

"Hooray for Looey!" shouted Red. "A bull's-eye! Shoot again!"

Freddy, peering out from his hiding-place, was so excited he could hardly breathe. Here was real work for a detective, and no mistake. For these men were certainly robbers. And if he could capture them, his name as a detective was made.

But just then, as Looey was whizzing for the tenth time up into the tree-tops, one of the ropes broke; he let go his hold and went up in a great curve like a rocket, then came hurtling down through the foliage and into

the very bush behind which Freddy was hiding.

He wasn't hurt, for the bush had broken his fall, and he picked himself up immediately, and his eye fell on the amazed pig. Freddy did not wait to see what would happen. With a squeal of fright he bolted.

"A pig! Quick, Red, a nice fat pig!" shouted Looey, and started after him, the

73

other robber close behind. There was much shouting and a great banging of revolvers, and two or three bullets whizzed past Freddy's head, but he was a good runner and in a very few minutes had left them far behind.

He ran on for a while, then sat down to rest under a beech-tree—and realized suddenly that he didn't know where he was. The woods on this side of the creek extended for many miles. If he could find the creek, he would be all right—but he did not know where the creek was. And the day was cloudy; he could not tell his direction from the position of the sun. "Well, I suppose the best thing to do is to keep on going," he said to himself. "May meet a squirrel or a jay who can tell me where I am." And he started on.

But though he walked and walked, he met no one, and there was no sign of the creek. He had just about decided that he would have to stay out all night when he noticed

74

some footprints. "H'm, someone been along here not many minutes ago," he said. "Looks like a pig, too. Wonder what another pig is doing in these woods. I guess I'll follow them and see if I can catch up."

So he went on, following the footprints, until he came to a place where the other pig had sat down to rest before going on. There was the plain print of a curly tail in the leaf mould under a beech-tree. Freddy sat down too, and then suddenly something about the place seemed familiar to him. This beech-tree, those bushes over there—"Why, this is where I sat down to rest myself a long time ago! Those are my own footprints I've been following!"

This realization made him feel very foolish, as well it might, for it *is* rather silly for a detective to try to shadow himself. Still, he realized that all he had to do was to follow those footprints *backward* instead of forward, and he would come out by the hermit's house. Which he did, and presently he heard the sound of voices.

But this time he did not stop to see what the robbers were doing. He gave the house a wide berth, jumped into the creek, swam across, and in a few minutes more was back on familiar ground.

"I'll just stop in and see if anything has been heard of Egbert," he said to himself. So he turned down toward the Widow Winnick's home. Half a dozen small rabbits were playing about on the edge of the woods as he came up, and one of them called down the rabbit-hole: "Mother! Mr. Freddy's here!"

Almost at once Mrs. Winnick's head popped up through the opening. But it was a changed Mrs. Winnick that beamed happily at him.

"Oh, Mr. Freddy!" she cried. "How can I ever thank you? My Egbert! You found him for me!"

"But," stammered the bewildered Freddy,

"I didn't—" And then he stopped. For one of the little rabbits who were standing around him in a respectful and admiring circle hiccuped, and said politely: "Excuse me." And Freddy saw it all. Of course! That rabbit had been Egbert all the time!

He recovered himself just in time. "Oh, don't thank me, Mrs. Winnick. Don't thank me," he said rather grandly. "It was nothing, I assure you—nothing at all. Indeed, I am very grateful to you for having sent me down in that direction, for I have made some very important discoveries. However, I am glad Egbert got back safely. All the other children are well, I hope. Good, good; I am very glad to hear it. Good evening." And he went on homeward.

"Well," he said to himself, "I guess as a detective I'm not so bad after all. Restored a lost child to his mother and discovered a band of robbers, all in one day! Huh, Sherlock Holmes never did more than that, I bet. And now for those rats!"

CHAPTER V

THE CASE OF PRINNY'S DINNER

FREDDY was a pretty busy pig for the next few weeks, Mrs. Winnick told all her friends about how quickly he had found Egbert, and her friends told other animals, and they all praised him very highly. At first Freddy tried to explain. He said that he really hadn't done anything at all, and that he didn't even know that the rabbit he had sent home was Egbert. But everyone said: "Oh, you just talk that way because you are so modest," and they praised him more highly than ever.

And they brought him detective work to do. Most of them were simple cases, like Egbert's, of young animals that had run away from home or got lost. But a number of them were quite important. There was, for instance, the strange case of Prinny's dinner. Prinny was a little white woolly dog who lived with Miss Mary McMinnickle in a little house a mile or so down the road. Prinny was a nice dog, in spite of his name, of which he was very much ashamed. His whole name was Prince Charming, but Miss McMinnickle called him Prinny for short. Now Prinny's dinner was always put out for him on the back porch in a big white bowl. Sometimes Prinny was there when it was put out, and then he ate it and everything was all right. But sometimes he would be away from home when Miss McMinnickle put it out, and he would come back an hour or two later and the bowl would be empty.

"The funny part of it is," he said to Freddy, "that there isn't ever a sign of any animal having been near it. I wish you'd see what you can do about it."

So Freddy took the case. First he got some flour and sprinkled it around on the porch, but though the food was gone from the bowl when he and Prinny came back later, there were no footprints to be seen. Then he watched for two afternoons, hidden behind the back fence with his eye at a knot-hole. But on these days the dinner was not touched.

"Have you any idea who it is?" asked Prinny anxiously. The poor little dog was getting quite thin.

"H'm," said Freddy; "yes. It's narrowing down, it's narrowing down. Give me another day or two and I think we'll have him."

Now, this time Freddy wasn't just looking wise and pretending, for he really did have an idea. The next day, before the sun had come up, he went down to Miss Mc-Minnickle's. He took with him Eeny and

Quik, two of the mice who lived in the barn, and they hid under the back porch. The mice were very proud that Freddy had asked them to help him, so they didn't mind the long wait, and they all played "twenty questions" and other guessing games until finally, late in the afternoon, they heard Miss McMinnickle come out on the porch and set down the bowl containing Prinny's dinner.

"Quiet now, boys," said Freddy. "I told Prinny to stay up at the farm until after dark, so the thief will think that there's no one here."

For half an hour they waited. Then, without any warning, without any sound of cautious footsteps on the floor of the porch close over their heads, there was a rattling sound, as if someone were tapping the bowl with a stick. The mice looked at Freddy in alarm, but he winked reassuringly at them. "They're there," he said. "Wait here till I call you." And he crawled quickly out from under the porch.

Three crows were perched on the edge of the big bowl, gobbling down Prinny's dinner as fast as they could. At sight of Freddy they flew with a startled squawk up into the

branches of a tree, from which they glared down at him angrily.

"Aha!" said the detective. "Caught you at it, didn't I? Ferdy, I didn't think it of you, stealing a poor little dog's dinner! I knew it was some kind of bird when we didn't find any footprints and when hiding behind the fence wasn't any good. I suppose you saw me from the air, eh? But I thought it would be some of those thieving jays from the woods. I didn't expect to find *you* here, Ferdy."

Ferdinand, the oldest of the crows, who had been Freddy's companion on the trip to the north pole the year before, merely grinned at his friend. "Aw, you can't prove anything, pig," he said. "Who's going to believe you? It's just your word against mine."

"Is that so!" exclaimed Freddy. "Well, I've got witnesses, smarty. Come out, boys," he called, and the two mice came out and sat on the edge of the porch.

Ferdinand looked a little worried at this. He was caught, and all the animals would soon know about it. Of course, they couldn't do anything to him. But they would be angry at him, and it isn't much fun living with people who don't approve of your actions, even if they can't punish you for them. In fact, it is often much pleasanter, when you have done something you shouldn't, to be punished and get it over with. Ferdinand

84

thought of this, and he also thought of his dignity. He had always been a very dignified crow, and it certainly wasn't very dignified to be caught stealing a little dog's dinner.

So he flew down beside the pig. "Oh, come, Freddy," he said; "it was just a joke. Can't we settle this out of court? We'll promise not to do it again if you won't say anything about it."

"Well, that's up to Prinny," said the pig. "It doesn't seem like a very good joke to him. But I'll talk to him about it. You three crows had better not be here when he gets back, though."

"All right," said Ferdinand. "That's fair enough. Do the best you can for us, Freddy. We'll push off now."

"Hey, wait a minute," said one of the other crows. "How about these mice? How do we know they won't talk?"

"Say, listen," squeaked Eeny shrilly. "Just because we're small, you think we haven't got any sense, you big black useless noisy feather-headed bug-eaters, you!" His anger at the insult was so hot that he fairly danced about the porch on his hind legs. "Another one like that and I'll climb that tree and gnaw your tail-feathers off!"

"Oh, he didn't mean anything, Eeny," said Ferdinand, edging a little away from the enraged mouse. "Sure, we know you won't say anything."

"Well, let him keep a civil tongue in his head, then," grumbled Eeny. "Come on, Quik." And he started off home without waiting for Freddy.

The pig overtook them, however, a minute later, and they climbed up on his back, for it was slow going for such small animals across the fields. "I must say, Freddy," remarked Quik, "that I think you're letting the crows off pretty easy."

Freddy nodded. "Yes, that's the trouble with this detective business. You see, there isn't much of anything else to do. Of course with Ferdinand, I'm sure he'll let Prinny alone now. He really did think it was more of a joke than anything else. But if he wanted to keep on stealing things, there isn't anything I could do to stop him. We ought to have a jail, that's what we ought to have."

"You mean like the one in Centerboro?" asked Eeny.

"Yes. Then when we find any animal doing anything he shouldn't, we could lock him up for a while."

"You mean if a cat chased us, he could be locked up in the jail?" asked the mice. And when Freddy said yes, that was exactly what he did mean, they both agreed that a jail was certainly needed.

So that evening Freddy called a meeting of all the animals in the cow-barn, where the

three cows, Mrs. Wiggins and Mrs. Wurzburger and Mrs. Wogus, lived. It was one
of the finest cow-barns in the county, for
when the animals had come back from
Florida with a buggyful of money that they
had found, Mr. Bean had been so grateful
that he had fixed up all the stables and
houses they lived in in the most modern
style, with electric lights and hot and cold
water and curtains at the windows, and
steam heat in the winter-time. Even the hen-
house had all these conveniences and such
little extra comforts as electric nest-warmers,
and little teeters and swings and slides for
the younger chickens.

All the animals on the neighboring farms
as well as at Mr. Bean's had by this time
heard about Freddy's success as a detective,
so the meeting was a large one. A lot of the
woods animals, including Peter, the bear,
came. There were even a few sheep, and if
you know anything about sheep, you will

realize how much interest the proposal for a jail had created, for there is nothing harder than to interest sheep in matters of public policy. Freddy found it unnecessary to make much of a speech, for nearly all of his audience agreed at once that the jail would fill, as Charles, the rooster, aptly expressed it, a long-felt want. Practically the only dissenting voice was that of Jinx. When Freddy threw the meeting open to discussion, Jinx jumped to his feet.

"I don't see what we want a jail for," he said. "We've always got along well enough without one before."

"We got along without nice places to live in, too," replied Freddy. "But it's nice to have them."

"Yes, but we aren't going to live in the jail."

"Some of us are," said Freddy significantly.

"You mean animals like the rats, I suppose," returned the cat. "Well, if you're such a swell detective, why don't you catch them and get Everett's train back? If you aren't any smarter at catching other animals that steal things than you have been about them, you won't have anybody in your old jail. And anyway I don't see any need for it. Let me get hold of those rats and you won't need any jail to put 'em in."

"I'll catch 'em all right," said Freddy. "Even Sherlock Holmes couldn't do every-thing in a minute. These things take time. I guess I've settled quite a number of cases since I started being a detective, haven't I?"

"Sure he has! Shut up, Jinx!" shouted the other animals, and Jinx had to sit down.

So the matter was voted upon, and it was decided by a vote of seventy-four to one that there should be a jail. But where? After a long discussion the meeting agreed that the two big box stalls in the barn would be a good place. Mr. Bean's three horses lived in the barn, but they had stalls near the door, and the box stalls were never used.

"How do you feel about it, Hank?" asked Freddy.

Hank was the oldest of the horses, and he was never very sure of anything except that he liked oats better than anything in the world. "I don't know," he said slowly. "I guess it would be all right. Some animals would be all right, and then again, some wouldn't. I wouldn't want elephants or tigers. Or polar bears. Or giraffes. Or—"

"Or kangaroos or leopards or zebras," said Freddy impatiently. "We know that. But there won't be any animals of that kind."

"Oh, then I guess it'll be all right," said Hank. "These prisoners, they'd be company for me, too. I'd like that."

"That's all settled, then," said Freddy. "Hank can be jailer and look after the prisoners and see that they don't escape. Then let's see; we'll need a judge, to say how long the prisoners shall stay in jail. Now, I suggest that a good animal for that position would be—"

"Excuse me!" crowed Charles, the rooster, excitedly. "I'd like to speak for a moment, Mr. Chairman."

"All right," said Freddy. "Mr. Charles has the floor. What is it, Charles?"

Charles flew up to the seat of the buggy, and all the animals crowded closer. The rooster was a fine speaker and he used words so beautifully that they all liked to hear him, although they didn't always know what he was talking about. Neither did he, sometimes, but nobody cared, for, as with all good speakers, what he said wasn't half so important as the noble way he said it.

"Ladies and gentlemen," said Charles, "it is with a great sense of my own inadequacy that I venture to address this distinguished meeting. We have gathered here this evening to pay tribute to the genius—and I use the word 'genius' without fear of denial—of one of our number, a simple farm animal, who yet, by virtue of his great talents, his dogged determination, and his pleasing personality, has risen to a position of trust and responsibility never before occupied by any animal. I refer, ladies and gentlemen, to Freddy, the detective." He paused for the cheers, then continued. "It has been said of Freddy that 'he always gets his animal.' But his career is too well known to all of you for me to dwell upon its successive stages."—

"Yeah, I guess it is!" remarked Jinx sarcastically. "Why don't he get those rats then?"

"And," Charles continued without heed-

ing the interruption, "who am I to come before you with suggestions concerning a subject about which he to whom I refer knows
more than any living animal?"—

"I'll tell you who you are!" shouted the
cat, who was always thoroughly exasperated
by Charles's long-windedness. "You're a
silly rooster, and if Henrietta catches you up
there making a speech again, *she'll* make
some suggestions you won't like!"

"Shut up! Put him out!" shouted the animals, and Jinx subsided. But Charles was
seen to shiver slightly. For Henrietta, his
wife, didn't approve of his public speaking,
and she had been heard to threaten to pull
out the handsome tail-feathers he was so
proud of if she caught him at it again.

Presently, however, he recovered himself
and went on, though somewhat hurriedly.
"I do not wish to detain you unduly, so I will
proceed to the matter of which I wish to
speak: the matter of selecting a judge. Now,
it is not easy to be a judge. When the

prisoner is brought before the judge, he must hear all the facts in the case, and must first decide whether the prisoner is innocent or guilty. If guilty, he must then decide how long the prisoner ought to spend in jail. Now, this is not an easy task. Whoever becomes judge will have a great responsibility. He will, moreover, have very little time to himself. I feel sure that none of you animals will really want the position. But I have thought the matter over carefully, and I am willing to sacrifice myself for the public good. I wish to propose myself as judge."

He paused, while some of the animals applauded and some grumbled.

"As to my qualifications for the position," he went on, trying to look as modest as he could, which wasn't very much, "it is hardly seemly for me to speak. You know me, my friends; whether or not I possess the wisdom, experience, and honesty necessary for this great task I leave it to you to judge. I have lived among you for many years; my record may perhaps speak for itself. I can only say that if you express your confidence in me by electing me to office, I shall do my utmost, I shall spare no labor, to be worthy of the confidence you thus express in me." And he flew down from the buggy.

The meeting at once divided into two parties, one for Charles and one for Peter, the bear, who was Freddy's candidate. Most of the animals who knew Charles well were for Peter, for though they were fond of Charles, they didn't think much of his brains. "He talks too much, and he thinks too much about himself to make a good judge," they said. But those who didn't know him so well made the common mistake of thinking that because he spoke well, he knew a lot. They thought that Peter had brains too, but there was a serious drawback to Peter. From December to March he was always sound asleep in his cave in the woods, so that any cases that came up in the winter would have to wait over until spring. Some of the anti-Charles party said that didn't matter; a good judge asleep was better than a bad judge awake. But the general feeling was that it wouldn't be a good idea to elect a judge that slept nearly half the time.

A number of speeches were made, and the argument grew so bitter that most of the sheep went home, and two squirrels got to fighting in a corner and had to be separated before the voting could start. When the vote was counted, it was found that Charles had won.

The rooster wanted to make a speech of acceptance, and he flew back up on the buggy seat, but he had got no further than "My friends, I extend to one and all my heartiest thanks—" when Jinx, who had disappeared during the voting, stuck his head in the door.

"Hey, Charlie," he called; "Henrietta wants you."

Charles's sentence ended in a strangled squawk, and he jumped down and hurried outside. But Henrietta was not there. Charles looked around for a moment; then, deciding that Jinx had played a trick on him, he turned to go in, when a voice above him called: "Hi, judge! Here's a present for you!" And plop! plop! plop!—soft and squashy things hit the ground all around him. He dashed for the door, but he was a quarter of a second too late. An over-ripe tomato struck him fair on the back and flattened him to the ground, while peals of coarse laughter came from the roof.

He got up and shook himself. But it was no use. The handsome feathers he had cleaned and burnished so carefully for the meeting were damp and bedraggled. He could make no speech now; he couldn't even go back into the cow-barn. A fine plight for a newly elected judge! But he knew whom he had to thank for it. Jinx had got those mischievous coons from the woods to play this childish trick on him. And he'd get even with them, see if he didn't! They'd forgotten that he was a judge now. He'd put 'em in jail and keep 'em there, that's what he'd do. And half-tearfully muttering threats, the new judge, after a mournful glance back at the barn, where honor and applause awaited him in vain, stumbled off across the barnyard toward the hen-coop.

CHAPTER VI

THE DEFEAT OF SIMON'S GANG

On one side of the rail fence was a ditch, on the other was a cornfield. Between the corn and the fence was a lane, and down this lane Freddy was sauntering. Although it was a windless day, there were odd little rustlings and swishings all about him, and now and then a corn-stalk or a tuft of grass or a bush beside the fence would be shaken for a moment as if a breeze had passed over it. Freddy, however, did not seem to notice any of these things, but strolled along, stopping now and then, as a detective will, to examine a footprint or a stone or a mark on a fence rail.

Presently fence and lane and ditch turned sharply to the left. Freddy turned with them, but as soon as he was round the corner, he darted quickly aside into a tangle of bushes and vines in an angle of the fence. Here, completely hidden, he lay motionless for perhaps a minute. And then a rabbit hopped into sight. It hopped along quietly, peering about sharply, but it did not see the pig and went cautiously on. Following the rabbit came Clarence, the porcupine who lived up in the woods, creeping along and trying hard to keep his quills from rattling. A squirrel ran stealthily along the fence above Freddy's head, but so intent was he on keeping the porcupine in sight that he did not see the pig crouching below him. There was a rustling in the tall corn, and a goat stuck his head out, looked up and down the lane, then retreated as Robert, Mr. Bean's dog, came slinking along on the porcupine's trail.

"Very good," said Freddy to himself as he watched the animals go by. "Very good indeed. They're learning.—But good gracious!" he exclaimed as a sound of trampling and crashing came from the cornfield. "That can't be Mrs. Wiggins again. My, my! Mr. Bean *will* be mad!" He got up, just as the cow appeared in the lane, leaving behind her a broad path of trampled corn.

"Where are they, Freddy?" she panted. "I've been shadowing that Robert, but I guess I lost him again." She sat down heavily. "Whew! This is certainly trying work, being a detective! And hot! I'm going to pick a cool day next time I try it." She looked back at the trail she had beaten down. "I'm afraid I've spoiled one or two stalks of Mr. Bean's corn."

"One or two!" Freddy exclaimed. "My goodness, you've wrecked the whole field! Mr. Bean will be good and sore, and I don't blame him."

"Oh pshaw, Freddy," said the cow, "you

know perfectly well that you can't shadow anybody unless you hide from them, and an animal as big as I am can't hide behind one or two little spears of grass the way a cat or a dog can. And besides, you said yourself that an animal couldn't be a good detective without a lot of practice. What else could I do?"

"Why, you'll just have to give up being a detective, that's all," replied the pig. "At least that kind of detective. Because there's lots to detective work besides shadowing. You have to hunt for clues, too, and then think about them until you can figure out what they mean."

Mrs. Wiggins sighed heavily. "Oh dear!" she said. "You know thinking isn't my strong point, Freddy. I mean, I've got good brains, but they aren't the kind that think easily. They're the kind of brains that if you let 'em go their own way, they are as good as anybody's, but if you try to *make* them do anything, like a puzzle, they just won't work at all."

"Well," said Freddy, "detective work is a good deal like a puzzle. But I *do* think you ought not to try to do this shadowing. Mr. Bean certainly won't like having the corn spoiled this way, and he's been pretty touchy

lately anyway. Not that I blame him, now that all the animals have started to play detective all over the farm. I heard him tell Mrs. Bean that he was getting sick and tired of having about fifteen animals sneaking along behind him every time he leaves the house. And whenever he looks up from his work, he says, no matter where he is, there are eyes peering at him—dozens and dozens of eyes watching him from hiding-places."

"Ugh!" exclaimed the cow with a little shiver. "I know how that is! Nothing makes me more nervous than to have something watching me and not saying anything. I remember, when the rats used to live in our barn, that old Simon used to sit in his hole and just watch me without moving a whisker. Just did it to make me nervous. But excuse me, Freddy; I didn't mean to mention the rats."

"Oh, that's all right," said the pig. "I don't mind. Though I must confess I don't know just what to do about them. It's the only case so far that has given me much trouble."

"Nasty creatures!" exclaimed the cow. "If I could just get up in that loft, I'd show 'em!"

"I wish you could," said Freddy. "You could just pick the train up on one horn and walk off with it. But the stairs are too narrow. No, I've got to think out something else. Oh, I'll get an idea sooner or later."

"That's it," said Mrs. Wiggins. "Ideas! You've got to have 'em to be a detective. And I can't remember when I had my last one But land sakes, there must be some way of getting the train. Couldn't you tie a rope on it and pull it out?"

"H'm," said Freddy thoughtfully, "that's an idea."

"An idea!" exclaimed the cow. "Gracious, Freddy, that isn't an idea; it's just something I thought of."

"It's an idea all the same," said the pig, "and a good one. But we'd have to do it quick, or they'd gnaw the rope in two. Come on, walk back to the barn with me and talk it over. I'd like to get at it tonight if I can."

So they strolled back, talking so earnestly that they never noticed that they were being rather clumsily shadowed by half a dozen animals of assorted sizes who dodged behind trees and darted across open places like Indians on the war-path. Mrs. Wiggins was so excited to find that she had really had an idea after all, and so flattered that Freddy was actually asking for her advice, that she hardly looked where she was going, and Alice remarked to Emma as they passed: "I've rarely seen Mrs. Wiggins so animated. She looks quite flushed." "Humph!" replied Emma, who was a little upset that day because her Uncle Wesley had scolded her for eating minnows—"Humph! It always goes to her head when she gets a little attention!"

Jinx was up in the loft where he spent much of his time now, though there was very little he could do there but watch the train make its periodic trips to the grain-box and back and listen to the insults and ribald songs that the rats shouted at him. He came down at once when Freddy called him, and went into conference with the pig and the cow. And when they finally separated to go to supper, they had decided on a plan.

There was a door in the loft through

which Mr. Bean took in the hay every summer. Over the door was a beam with a pulley
at the end, and through the pulley ran a stout
rope that ended in an iron hook. The other
end of the rope came down into the loft,
where it was coiled upon the floor. Late that
evening, when Mr. Bean had finished the
chores and had gone round to the barns and
the hen-house and the pig-pen and turned
out the lights and said good night to the animals in his gruff, kindly way and had then
gone into the kitchen to eat a couple of apple
dumplings and a piece of pie and a few
doughnuts before going to bed, Freddy and
Jinx went up into the loft. The train was
still going back and forth, for although the
rats felt that they had completely outwitted
the cat, they were wise enough to realize that
the luck might turn any day, and they intended to lay away as big a supply of grain
as they could. So they worked in shifts, night
and day.

When they heard Freddy, who hadn't

visited the loft since the night when he had broken his tooth, they set up a derisive shout. "Yea! Here's old Freddy, old curly-tail! How's tricks, pig? Who you going to arrest tonight?" And then they began to sing:

"Oh, we are the gay young rats
    Who laugh at the barnyard prigs;
We can lick our weight in cats,
    And double our weight in pigs.

"We live wherever we like,
    We do whatever we please;
An enemy's threat can strike
    No fear to such hearts as these.

"When the pig detective squeals,
    When cats lash furious tails,
Our laughter comes in peals,
    And our laughter comes in gales.

"We've done as we always did,
    We do as we've always done,
Though cats and pigs forbid,
    For we take orders from none.

"So, cats and pigs and men,
    If you want to avoid a fuss,

Stay safely in house and pen
And don't interfere with us."

"Kind of like themselves, don't they?" remarked Jinx. Freddy said nothing, but went quickly to work. The loose end of the rope he threw out of the door to Mrs. Wiggins, who was waiting below, and then, after several trials, during which he nearly fell out himself, he got hold of the hook and drew it down into the loft.

The rats, meanwhile, in order to show their contempt for him, were marching all round the floor inside the train, shouting out their song at the top of their lungs. They felt pretty sure that neither of their enemies would make another direct attack, and they were so taken up with the effort to outdo one another in thinking up insulting new verses for the song that they didn't realize just what was going on. Suddenly Freddy said: "Let's go!" The two animals made a pounce for the train, and before the rats knew what had happened, the big hook was firmly fastened in the engine window, and Freddy had shouted to Mrs. Wiggins, who, with the other end of the rope looped about one horn, simply walked away from the barn.

There was a rattle and a great squeaking as the train was dragged across the floor. It reached the door, swung out, and was pulled

up toward the pulley, the rats dropping from it like peas from a pod. Jinx had run downstairs, and as the rats picked themselves up and ran for shelter, he was among them, cuffing and slapping. Simon, unfortunately, had not been in the train, but his son Ezra was there, and Jinx grabbed him by the back of the neck and held on while the others made their escape. Then Mrs. Wiggins walked back toward the barn and the train came down to the ground at the end of the rope.

The rats who had not been in the train, desperate at the loss of their means of livelihood, swarmed angrily out of their holes as their comrades were dragged squealing and struggling across the floor, and Freddy, feeling that his work there was completed, saw no reason for staying longer. In fact he fell down the last eight steps of the stairs, so eager was he to get away. But outside, by the captured train, he recovered himself and thanked Mrs. Wiggins generously for her part in the victory.

"Everett owes his train to you and no one else," he said. "You don't have to bother with learning to shadow people if you want to be a detective. Goodness, you've got *ideas*. That's the important thing."

"Ideas!" exclaimed the cow in bewilderment. "Why, land of love, that wasn't an idea! I never have ideas. I told you that."

"It certainly was an idea," protested the pig.

"Well, if that's what you want to call it . . . it just looked like common sense to me."

Freddy didn't say anything for a minute; then he turned his attention to the prisoner, who had given up struggling and was lying quiet under Jinx's paw. "Good work, Jinx," he said. "We got one of 'em, anyway. Better take him down and have the judge sentence him right away. Then we can lock him up in the jail."

"Aw, what do we want of a judge?" demanded the cat. "You leave him to me. I'll see he don't cause any more trouble." And he glared ferociously at Ezra.

But Freddy and Mrs. Wiggins insisted, and Jinx finally gave in. "Come on, then," he said. "I shouldn't have caught him if it hadn't been for you, so I guess you ought to have the say-so."

The hen-house was dark when they reached it, but at the first tap on the door a head popped out of a window and a cross voice wanted to know what they meant by waking up honest chickens in the middle of the night. "Go along about your business," scolded the voice, "or I'll call my husband, and *he'll* soon settle you."

Jinx grinned at the picture of Charles trying to drive away a cat and a pig and a cow, but he only said politely: "Excuse us, Henrietta, but this is a very important case that won't wait. We've got a prisoner here, and we must see the judge."

But Henrietta was not appeased. "I'm not going to have my sleep disturbed by a lot of roistering cats and pigs, and you needn't try any of your soft soap on me either, Jinx. I know you! And who's that out there with you—Mrs. Wiggins? Take shame to yourself, Mrs. Wiggins, to be gallivanting about

the country at all hours, like this, with a pack
of disreputable scalawags and good-for-
nothing disturbers of the peace—"

"Oh, come, Henrietta," boomed Mrs.
Wiggins good-naturedly, "I guess you know
me well enough so you don't think I'm up
to any mischief."

"Birds of a feather flock together," interrupted the hen. "I can only judge you by
the company you keep, ma'am. But of course
nothing *I* can say would do you any good—"

"Oh, call Charles, will you?" demanded
Freddy impatiently. "We've captured a prisoner and we want to have the judge sentence
him."

"Give him six months," came the sleepy
voice of the rooster from within the coop.

"Why, you don't even know who it is or
what he's done!" exclaimed Mrs. Wiggins.
"Come out, now, Charles, and do your duty
as you said you would when you were
elected."

"Give him a year, then," came the sleepy

voice again. "And take him away. I want to go to sleep."

"There, you've got your answer," said Henrietta. "Now go along and stop your racket. What'll people think?"

"I know what they'll think," said Freddy angrily. "They'll think we've got to get another judge. You wouldn't elect Peter because you said he slept half the year. How about a judge that won't stay awake long enough after his election to hear the first case that comes up? Come on, animals; we'll go get Peter."

But this didn't suit the hen at all. She was very proud of having her husband a judge, though she wouldn't have let him know it for anything, and with a hurried "Wait a minute," she disappeared inside.

There was a rustling and flapping, a squawk or two, and then the door opened and a very sleepy Charles stood before them. "Wha's all this?" he demanded. "Very incos— inconsiderate, I call it." His tongue was thick with sleep, and he leaned against the door-post and closed his eyes.

But a sharp peck from his wife roused him, and he frowned at the prisoner. "What's he done?" he demanded.

They told their story, and when it was finished, Charles, finally awake, turned to

Ezra. "Is there any reason why you shouldn't go to jail, prisoner?" he asked.

The rat started to say something, looked up craftily at Jinx, who held a heavy paw in readiness, and, lowering his eyes, said meekly: "No, sir."

"Nothing to say for yourself, eh?" said

the judge. "Well, it's your first offense—or, rather, it's the first time you've been caught, so I'm going to give you a light sentence. Three months in jail. And now I want to say to you, prisoner, that I hope you'll do some serious thinking during those three months. I hope you'll see the wisdom of living at peace with your fellow animals and of letting other people's property alone. I want to say to you—"

But, whatever else it was that he wanted to say, it was lost to the world, for at that moment Henrietta, who had little patience for speeches at any time, and none at all for them in the middle of the night, seized him by the tail-feathers, yanked him inside, and slammed the door.

CHAPTER VII

A CRIME WAVE IN THE BARNYARD

FREDDY was now a made pig. His victory over Simon's gang and the return of the stolen train to Everett brought him a great many cases. He took Mrs. Wiggins into partnership, and it was an excellent combination, he supplying the ideas and she the common sense, neither of which is of much use without the other. They themselves handled only the more difficult cases, turning over the simpler ones to their staff, which consisted of several smaller animals who were good at shadowing and gathering information. Freddy printed a large sign and hung it on the shed which had once been the offices of Barnyard Tours, Inc. It read:

FREDERICK & WIGGINS
DETECTIVES

Plain and fancy shadowing. Stolen articles restored. Criminals captured. Missing animals found and returned to bosoms of families. Our unexcelled record makes it worth your while to investigate. Not a loss to a client in more than a century.

Mrs. Wiggins objected at first to the last sentence. "We haven't been in business but a week," she said.

"What difference does that make?" asked Freddy. "It's true, isn't it?"

She had to admit that it was. "But, don't you see, it sounds as if we'd been detectives for a long time."

"That's just the way I want it to sound," replied the pig.

So Mrs. Wiggins didn't say any more.

Pretty soon there were eight animals in

the jail. There was Ezra, and there were two rabbits who had stolen some parsnips, and there was a goat named Eric, who had come to the farm to visit his friend Bill and had eaten Mrs. Bean's filet lace table-cloth and Mr. Bean's best night-shirt right off the clothes-line. Then there were two snails who had come up on Mrs. Bean's freshly scrubbed front porch one night and left little shiny trails all over it. And there was a tramp cat who had chased Henrietta up into a tree one day when she was out calling. And finally there was a horse-fly named Zero.

The capture of this fly had been a difficult matter. The two dogs, Jock and Robert, who had been appointed policemen, could of course do nothing about it. Zero was not an ordinary fly who bit and flew away. He had attached himself to Mrs. Wogus. He lived in the cow-barn, and as soon as it was light in the morning, he started biting her. When she went down to the pasture, he followed along and bit her some more. He was very agile, and when she swished her tail at him, he only laughed. Even when she climbed down into the duck-pond and lay in the water with only the tip of her nose showing, he would fly down and bite her nose. It got so bad that she appealed to Freddy.

Now, every night Zero slept on the ceiling of the cow-barn. He was right over Mrs. Wogus, so that as soon as it was light enough for him to see, he could drop down without wasting a second and begin biting. "Perfectly simple matter, Mrs. W.," said Freddy in his business-like way. "Just you leave it to me." And he went into the house and borrowed a piece of fly-paper from Mrs. Bean and put it in the cow-barn. "That'll do the business," he said.

Early the next morning he was awakened by a great commotion, and he ran out and saw a crowd of animals gathered about the cow-barn. He hurried up to them importantly. "Where's the prisoner?" he demanded.

They made way for him and he saw, struggling feebly in the sticky paper, not Zero, but Eeny, who had gone into the barn to see Mrs. Wiggins and, knowing nothing about the trap, had walked straight into it.

With some difficulty, and after getting a good deal of stickiness on his own snout,

Freddy rescued the unfortunate mouse, while Zero buzzed round impudently overhead. After listening to all the unpleasant things that Eeny's family had to say to him, the pig went outside to think. Undoubtedly he'd have to try something different now. And he was wondering what it would be when he gave a sharp squeal and jumped into the air. Something had stung him on the ear.

He looked around angrily, and there was Zero circling above his head, and a thin, whining laughter came down to him. "That's something for *you*, pig, in exchange for the fly-paper," buzzed Zero. "It'll be worse next time, so better leave me alone." And he flew off in search of Mrs. Wogus.

But Freddy had no intention of being intimidated by a fly. He got some jam and put it on Mrs. Wogus's nose. "Now," he said, "get into the pond with just your nose showing. Then when Zero lights, duck under the water for a minute. His feet will be stuck so he can't get away and he'll be drowned and that'll be the end of *him*."

So Mrs. Wogus went into the water, and Freddy sat down on the bank to watch. Zero was not in sight for the moment, and Freddy started thinking how clever he was, and then he got to thinking how comfortable he was, and his head nodded and nodded—and he woke up suddenly with a squeal of pain, for Zero had quietly alighted on his snout and bitten him ferociously.

"There's another for you, pig," droned the fly as he swooped over the enraged Freddy's head. "Maybe now you'll let me alone. I don't eat jam. It makes me fat, and a fly can't afford to be fat and slow on his wings these days. Too many birds and wasps around. But pigs! Why, Freddy, you couldn't catch a blind fly with one wing. No, sir, you—"

But Freddy, although he was hopping mad, was too good a detective to pay much attention to empty insults. Zero's words had given him an idea. Off he went at a fast trot, stopping only now and then to rub his smarting nose in the cool grass, and presently he was talking to a family of wasps who were building a new house under the eaves of the barn.

"It's a bad time to ask our help now," said the father wasp when he had heard what

Freddy wanted. "We've got this house on our hands, and the days are getting shorter all the time. Still—I might let you have George. Hey, George!"

George was a husky young wasp who was only too glad of any excuse to get away from house-building. Wasps build their houses of chewed-up leaves and things, and George had chewed until his jaws were lame. He listened to Freddy's instructions and then flew off toward the pasture. The pig trotted along after him.

When they reached the pasture, Mrs. Wogus was not in sight, and Freddy remembered uneasily that he had forgotten to tell her to come out of the pond. Good gracious, she had been sitting there for over an hour now! Sure enough, there was her black nose, smeared with jam, making a queer little island in the water. He threw pebbles at her until she came up; then he explained.

Mrs. Wogus was rather vexed. "You ought to have told me," she said. "It's no fun sitting there in the mud and the cold. with nothing to do but shiver. And the way the minnows tickle you, you wouldn't believe! I do hope I haven't caught a cold."

But she soon got warm in the hot sun, and Freddy went over with her into the pasture to watch proceedings. Pretty soon Zero came buzzing along. But this time as he dropped down to settle on Mrs. Wogus's nose, he heard the deep drone of George's wings and hastily went into a nose dive, flew right under the cow, then dashed off with the wasp in hot pursuit. It was like an airplane battle, with Zero dodging and twisting and George trying to get above him and drop on him, but it didn't last long, and presently Zero was driven down to the ground, where he took refuge in a small hole under a stone. George tried to go in after him, but the hole was too small.

"I'll dig him out," said Freddy. "You stand by to chase him again."

So Freddy turned the stone over, and up

buzzed Zero into the air, and the chase was on again. But this time when the fly was driven down, he went into a crevice in the stone foundation of the barn.

"You can't turn that over," said George. "Guess you'd better give up for today. Some time when I haven't got so much to do, I'd like nothing better than to catch that insect

for you, but I ought to get back now. Father won't like it."

"Wait," said Freddy; "I've got an idea. You watch till I come back."

He went into the barn, and in a few minutes came out with the two spiders, Mr. and Mrs. Webb, who were great friends of his.

In no time at all they had woven a web over the entrance of the crevice, and then they had Zero safe and fast. After that there was nothing for the fly to do but surrender, so he came out and the Webbs tied his feet and wings together, and Freddy carried him off to jail.

Freddy was very much pleased when they had eight prisoners in the jail. He wasn't so much pleased when, a week after the capture of Zero, they had thirty-four. "I don't understand it," he said to Mrs. Wiggins. "I suppose it must be one of these crime waves we read about."

"We'll have to enlarge the jail, at this rate," said Mrs. Wiggins.

"There'll be more animals inside than out," said Freddy.

They were strolling down through the pasture, and a number of strange animals passed them, going toward the barnyard. At last one, a motherly-looking Jersey cow, stopped and asked the way to the jail.

Freddy pointed it out to her. "Nothing wrong, I hope?" he said. "I mean, none of your family or friends are—er—*in*, are they?"

"Oh no," said the cow. "But I've heard of those poor animals locked up in jail, and I *do* feel so sorry for them, poor things! It's just *dreadful* not to be able to get out in the fresh air among their friends."

"If they'd behaved themselves, they wouldn't be there," said Freddy.

"Oh yes, I know," said the cow, "but it's so horrible to be locked up, isn't it? It makes me quite sad to think of them." And a tear rolled down her broad cheek.

"As a matter of fact, they have a pretty easy time," put in Mrs. Wiggins. "Play games and lie round and get lots to eat. I don't think you need be so sorry for them."

"I suppose it *is* silly of me," replied the other, "but I've always been that way. Anyone in trouble just wrings my heart strings. And it's better to be too tender-hearted, I always say, than to run the risk of getting too hard. Don't you think so?"

"Oh, undoubtedly," said Freddy. "But I wouldn't get very tender-hearted about that bunch of prisoners. They're a tough lot."

"Well," said the cow, "perhaps you're right. But I thought I'd just go down and see if there wasn't anything I could do to make things easier for them. I can't bear to think of them being unhappy. It hurts me here." And she tapped her left side with her right front hoof.

When the cow had gone on, Freddy said: "That's one reason—all these sentimental animals that come to visit the jail and feel sorry for the prisoners and want to do things for them. After all, they're there to be punished, not to have a good time. And we treat 'em well. There's no reason to cry over them and bring them better food than they ever get at home.—Why, what are you get-ting so red for?" he demanded suddenly.

For a blush had overspread Mrs. Wiggins's large face.

You have probably never seen a cow blush. And indeed the sight is unusual. There are two reasons for this. One is that cows are a very simple people, who do whatever they feel like doing and never realize that sometimes they ought to be embarrassed. You might think that they lack finer feelings. And in a way they do. They are not sensitive. But they are kind and good-natured, and if sometimes they seem rude, it is only due to their rather clumsy thoughtlessness.

The other reason is that cows' faces are not built for blushing. But as Mrs. Wiggins was so talented above her sisters in other directions, it is not to be marveled at that she could blush very handsomely.

Her flush deepened as Freddy spoke. "Why, I—now that you speak of it," she stammered, "I see that you're right, but—well, Freddy—land's sakes, I might as well confess it to you—I got to feeling sorry for those prisoners myself yesterday, especially those two goats. It seemed such a pity they couldn't be jumping round on the hills instead of sweltering in that hot barn. And I went out and got them a nice bunch of thistles for their supper."

Freddy frowned. "That's it!" he exclaimed. "That's just it! Sentimentality, that's what's going to ruin our jail. I *did* think, Mrs. W., that you had more sense!"

The cow looked a little angry. "If I knew what you were talking about," she said stiffly, "perhaps I might agree with you."

"Being sentimental?" said Freddy. "I'll tell you what it is. It's going round looking for someone or something to cry over, just for the fun of crying. You knew you weren't doing those goats any good. You just wanted to have a good time feeling sorry."

The nice thing about Mrs. Wiggins was that she always admitted it when she was wrong. She did so now after she had thought about it for a few minutes. "I guess you're right, Freddy," she said. "I won't do it again. —But, good grief, what's that rabbit up to?"

Freddy had noticed the rabbit too. It had hopped out of the long grass, turned and looked straight at them, then deliberately went into the garden where Mr. Bean grew lettuce and radishes and other vegetables and began nibbling at a head of lettuce. Now, no animals were allowed in this garden except the head squirrel and his gang, who did the weeding and could be trusted not to eat the vegetables. So Freddy was greatly shocked by such bold behavior.

"Come, come!" he shouted, hurrying up to the rabbit. "You're a bold one, I *must* say! You just come along with me. You're under arrest."

"Yes, sir," said the rabbit meekly. "Do we go to jail right away?"

"Jail?" said Freddy. "I guess we do go to jail, just as soon as the judge can sentence you."

The rabbit looked quite pleased at this and started hopping off, his mouth still full of lettuce leaves.

"Stop!" called Freddy, hurrying after him. "No use your trying to escape. Better come along quietly. You'll just make matters worse for yourself if you don't."

"I wasn't trying to escape," said the rabbit. "I was just starting for the hen-house so I could be sentenced.—I really was, sir," he added, as Freddy stared at him in amazement.

The pig was rather puzzled. The rabbit was evidently telling the truth, and yet such eagerness to be punished didn't seem reasonable. "You're a queer one," said Freddy. "I don't believe you understand. You've been stealing lettuce, and it's against the rules, and you're going to be punished by being sent to jail."

"But I *do* understand, sir," replied the prisoner. "I know I've done wrong, and—well, sir, I think I *ought* to be punished. As a lesson to me, sir. I ought to know better than to do such things."

"H'm," said Freddy, "you're saying all the things *I* ought to say. Still, they're true, and I'm glad you see it. Only if you feel that way, I can't see why you stole the lettuce in the first place."

"I can tell you that," said the rabbit. "But —well, I'd rather wait until after I'm sentenced."

"All right," said the pig. "And I'll do my best with the judge to see that your sentence isn't a long one. I'm sure you won't do it again."

"Oh, yes I shall!" exclaimed the rabbit anxiously. "Yes, sir, I'm apt to do things like that any time. I'm quite a desperate character, sir, really I am. You'd better get me a good long sentence."

"Say, look here!" said Freddy sharply. "Are you trying to make fun of me, or what? If you're a good law-abiding rabbit, as you seem to be, I can understand your being sorry that you'd done wrong and thinking that you ought to be punished. But I don't believe that anybody, animal or human, ever thought that he ought to be punished *a lot*. Come on, now, tell me the truth!"

At this the rabbit broke down and began to cry. "Oh dear!" he sobbed. "I thought it would be so easy to get into jail! I thought all you had to do was steal something. And I wanted to go to jail—the animals there all have such a good time, and don't have to work, and they play games and sing songs all day long, and other animals are sorry for them and bring them lots of good things to eat! Oh, please, Mr. Freddy, take me to the judge and get me a good long sentence."

"I'll do nothing of the kind," said Freddy

crossly. "And, what's more, I'm not going to arrest you at all. I'm going to give your ears a good boxing"—which he did while the rabbit submitted meekly—"and then you can go. Only let me tell you something. Don't go stealing any more lettuce in the hope that you'll be sent to jail. Because you won't. You'll get something you won't like at all."

"Wh—what's that?" sniveled the rabbit.

"I don't know," said Freddy. "I'll have to think up something. But you can bet it'll be something good."

Then he went back to where Mrs. Wiggins was waiting for him. "Can you beat it?" he exclaimed. "Did you hear that?"

"I certainly did," said the cow. "I tell you, Freddy, something's got to be done, and done quick. Let's go have a talk with Charles. Maybe he can suggest something."

CHAPTER VIII

THE JUDGE DISAPPEARS

THEY found the hen-house in a great state of excitement. A flock of young chickens— Henrietta's gawky, long-legged daughters —were crowding about their mother or dashing in and out on errands, and the older hens were running round distractedly, squawking and clucking, some of them bringing water in their beaks to sprinkle over one of their sisters, who had fainted, others merely hurrying aimlessly out of the door to stop and give several loud squawks and then hurry as aimlessly inside again.

At first the two detectives could get no answers to their questions in the general hubbub, but at last Freddy, losing patience, squeezed his way inside, seized Henrietta by a wing and pulled her over into a corner. "Come, now; what's the trouble here?" he demanded. "Pull yourself together, hen, and tell me what's wrong."

Henrietta glared at him for a moment without seeming to see him. Then suddenly she seemed to recognize him, and burst out wildly: "You!" she cried. "You *dare* come here, you wretched pig, with your fine airs and your lordly ways—you that's to blame for all this, you and all your smart friends that told him how fine it would be to be a judge! *You* are the one that got him into this, you imitation detective, you; you big chunk of fat pork!"

Freddy backed away a little. "Come, come, Henrietta," he said soothingly. "Let's not talk about me. I may be everything you say, but that doesn't get us anywhere, does it? I don't even know what's the matter yet."

But Henrietta's rage was quickly spent. She broke down and began to cry. "He's gone!" she sobbed. "My Charles, the finest husband a hen ever had! They've got him, my good, kind, noble Charles!"

Serious as the situation seemed, Freddy had to repress a grin. When Charles was around, Henrietta did nothing but scold him and tell him what a silly rooster he was. Outside the hen-house there was a strange whining, grumbling sound, and Freddy recognized it as Mrs. Wiggins's giggle. But fortunately the hen did not hear it and went on with her story.

There wasn't very much of it. Charles had been missing since late the previous afternoon None of the animals on the farm had seen him.

Freddy suggested the only thing he could think of. "He may have gone visiting," he said, "and been invited to stay all night."

"He wouldn't *dare* stay out all night!" flashed the hen. "Just let him try it once!" Then she began to cry again. "No, he's gone. It's one of those animals he sentenced to jail. There were a couple of them that said they'd get even with him when they got out. And now they've gone and done it. And I shall never see him again! Oh, my poor Charles! My noble husband!" And she flopped round in a violent fit of hysterics.

Freddy shook his head dolefully and went outside. "Come on," he said to the cow. "Nothing more to be got out of her. We'd better get busy right away. Now, where in the world do you suppose he can be?"

"Off somewhere having a good time probably," replied Mrs. Wiggins. "Though it *is* funny. Henrietta would peck his eyes out if he stayed out a minute after ten o'clock."

"Yes," said Freddy, "and none of the animals he has sentenced to jail have got out yet, so it can't be that. Of course, he might have been carried off by a hawk, or had a fight with a stray cat. But, for all his bluster and boasting, Charles is too clever to be caught like that. I expect we'd better put the whole force on it to go round and find out all they can."

So they got all their helpers together and sent them out in different directions to ask questions and look for signs of the missing rooster. Both Freddy and Mrs. Wiggins went out too. But when they met again late that evening, nothing had been found. Charles had vanished without leaving so much as a feather behind.

The next morning Freddy was up and out before the dew was off the grass, for this, he felt, was a case on which his reputation as a detective rested. It wasn't just an ordinary disappearance. Charles was the judge, an important personage, and if he wasn't found, and quickly, nobody would bring any more cases to the detectives.

He was on his way down to the cow-barn to get Mrs. Wiggins when he heard a loud moo behind him and, turning, saw that animal galloping toward him as fast as she could come.

"Come with me over to the jail," she panted. "I've got something to show you. I went over there when I got up, to check over the prisoners and see that they were all there, because I thought some of them might have escaped and perhaps murdered Charles—though, goodness knows, none of 'em are mad at him for sentencing them. Quite the contrary. Just listen to them."

The sounds of shouts and laughter and songs greeted them as they approached. Hank, from his stall, turned a weary eye on them as they entered. "I do wish you would do something about this," he said. "I thought it was going to be company for me, having the jail here, but, my land! nobody wants company twenty-four hours a day! They just keep it up all night. I haven't had a wink of sleep for ten days."

Freddy nodded. "Yes, we'll have to make some other arrangements. This jail isn't a

punishment any more at all. But we'll talk about that later. What was it you wanted to show me?" he asked the cow.

Without speaking she led him to the door of one of the stalls, hooked the wooden pin out of the staple, and opened the door. Inside, some twenty animals and birds were crowded together. One group was in a circle, watching two rabbits doing gymnastic stunts. Another group, with their heads together, were singing "Sweet Adeline" with a great deal of expression. Mrs. Wiggins raised one hoof and pointed dramatically at a third group. In the center of it was the missing judge, declaiming at the top of his lungs.

"On with the dance!" declaimed Charles.

"Stop! Silence!" shouted Freddy, and Mrs. Wiggins stamped on the floor to get attention.

"Let joy be unconfined!" went on Charles dramatically. Then he saw the visitors, and his voice flattened out into a whisper.

Heads turned; the song died down; the groups broke up and surrounded the detectives.

Freddy pushed his way through them and confronted Charles. "What on earth does this mean?" he demanded. "What are you doing here? Don't you know that Henrietta is half crazy with worry?"

"Why I—I'm in jail," explained Charles

a little hesitantly; then, gaining courage at the immediate applause which this remark drew from his fellow prisoners: "Tell Henrietta I'm very sorry," he went on, "but I'm serving a six weeks' sentence, and I can't come home until my time's up."

"A sentence!" exclaimed Mrs. Wiggins. "But how can you be serving a sentence? You're the judge. Who can sentence you?"

"The judge!" said Charles triumphantly. "I'm the judge, and I sentenced myself!"

"What for?"

"Well, I'll tell you," said Charles, now thoroughly at ease. "You see, two or three years ago I stole something. It doesn't matter what it was. Well, then, when I was elected judge, that old crime worried me. Here I am, I thought, sentencing other animals to jail for crimes no worse than the one I committed, and yet *I* never served any sentence for it. It got on my nerves after a while. It didn't seem right, somehow. What right had I to set myself up as better than these other animals and punish them for things when I was no better myself? The only fair thing, it seemed to me, the only just thing, the only honest thing, the only noble thing, was to punish myself. And so I did. I'm serving my sentence now."

The other prisoners set up a cheer, but Freddy scowled. "Nonsense!" he exclaimed. "I'll tell you why you're here. You're sick of being nagged at by Henrietta. I don't blame you there—I shouldn't like it either. And so you thought this would give you an excuse to stay away from home and have a good time. But you can't get away with it, Charles. This jail isn't a club. It—"

"But I stole something, I tell you," insisted the rooster. "I'm only getting the punishment I deserve. I can't get out."

"You can and you're going to," said Freddy. "You never stole anything in your life. And how are you going to be of any use as a judge when you're in jail yourself?"

"I don't see why I won't," protested

Charles. "Bring the prisoners down here and I can sentence 'em just the same, can't I?"

"No, you can't," put in Mrs. Wiggins. "Come along, now. Henrietta's waiting for you."

"I'm not going," said Charles.

Freddy turned and winked secretly at the cow. "Oh, all right, then," he said. "Let him stay here. We'll just have to elect another judge, that's all. We'll get Peter. There's a lot of the animals thought he would be a better judge anyway, and there'll be plenty more now, when this gets out."

But this didn't suit the rooster either. "You can't do that!" he shouted, hopping up and down in his excitement. "You can't do that! I was elected, and you can't put me out that way."

"Oh, can't we?" said Freddy. "Don't you know that a judge loses his job when he goes to jail? We don't have to put you out. You're just *out*, anyway. Unless, of course, you decide that there was some mistake about it and take back your sentence."

For a few minutes the crestfallen rooster thought this over in silence. He was having a very good time in the jail. On the other hand, in jail he was really just one of the prisoners. And outside he was a judge,

looked up to and respected by the entire community. Still—there was Henrietta. He knew that no story he could fix up would go down with Henrietta. And what she'd say —he shivered to think of it.

"Come on," said Freddy. "Henrietta is taking on terribly. You don't want her to feel badly, do you? She misses you, Charles." And he repeated some of the things Henrietta had said, about how good and noble he was.

Charles looked up quickly. "She said *that*!" he exclaimed.

"She certainly did," said Mrs. Wiggins.

"Well, then, I guess—I guess I'd better go back," said the rooster. And he walked dejectedly out of the door and reluctantly took the path toward the hen-house.

That evening Freddy and Mrs. Wiggins were strolling down through the pasture, talking over the new problems that confronted them in their detective work. From the hen-house came the angry clucking and gabbling of Henrietta's voice, going on and on and punctuated occasionally with Charles's shrill squawks. They listened for a few minutes, then grinned at each other and walked on.

"It's really a swell joke on us," said Freddy. "We were looking for a missing rooster, and there he was in jail all the time

—the one place nobody'd ever look for him."

"We find 'em," said Mrs. Wiggins complacently. "Wherever they are, we find 'em."

Freddy grinned more broadly as a particularly agonized shriek came from the hen-house. "We'd have no trouble finding the judge tonight," he said. "I bet that's the last time he stays out all night."

"He won't have a tail-feather left by morning," said the cow.

CHAPTER IX
JINX IS INDICTED

ALTHOUGH Freddy had been successful with nearly all his detective cases, there were two things that bothered him a good deal. The rats were still in the barn, for one thing, and though they couldn't get to the grain-box any more without running the risk of being caught by Jinx, who was always on guard, they had stolen enough grain while they had the train of cars to keep them all the next winter. And, for another thing, the two robbers were still living in the hermit's house, and Freddy hadn't yet thought up a way of bringing them to justice. One of the

mice, Cousin Augustus, had volunteered to
go live in the house with them, and the reports he brought back were disturbing.
They spent the day sleeping, or shooting at
the chimney, or mending their clothes. But
every night they went out and got in an
automobile and drove off, coming back in
the early morning with big packages of
dollar bills, which they kept in an old trunk
in the attic. They did all their own work—
even made their own clothes—but the house,
said Cousin Augustus, who was used to
Mrs. Bean's neat housekeeping, was a dis-
grace. "Dirty," he said, "isn't the word for
it! Crumbs all over the floor, and the stuffing
coming out of the sofa, and the kitchen sink
full of dirty dishes. And the window-cur-
tains simply black! You'd think they'd have
some pride!"

Cousin Augustus had succeeded in gnawing a hole through the back of the trunk and
in pulling out a package of the dollar bills,
which he had brought to Freddy. Nothing

would be easier, he said, than to take a gang of mice up there some night and get all the bills; but Freddy decided that there wasn't much point in this, as they didn't know whom the money had been stolen from, and so couldn't give it back to its owners. And certainly a pig-pen was no place for it. But he kept the package Cousin Augustus had brought, hoping that some day he might get a clue which would lead to the arrest of the robbers and the return of the money.

And then one morning, when Freddy was in his office, he heard a buggy draw up in the road opposite it, and, looking through the window, he saw two men lean out and read the sign he had printed. The man who was driving was the sheriff, who lived up near Centerboro. He was in his shirt-sleeves and had a tuft of thin gray whiskers on his chin and a silver star on his vest, and Freddy knew him well because he owned some pigs who were distant relatives of Freddy's. The other was a rather cross-looking man with a hard face, who had the stump of a cigar so firmly clamped between his teeth that it looked as if it was a part of his face.

"It may seem funny to *you*," the sheriff was saying, "you being from the city an' all, but I tell you these animals are *different*. They take trips to Florida in the winter, and they do all the work round the place without anybody tellin' 'em what to do, and there ain't one of 'em, so Mr. Bean tells me, that can't read."

"Bah!" exclaimed the hard-faced man so disgustedly that he almost lost his cigar stump. "I never heard such nonsense! You country hicks will believe anything. You can't tell me any animal can learn to read, to say nothing of setting up in the detective business and hanging out a sign. Who printed that sign for 'em? I suppose you'll tell me the animals did it!"

"Sure, they did it!" replied the sheriff. "I tell you, these animals are a lot smarter than some folks I know."

"Meanin' me?" said the other threateningly.

"I name no names," said the sheriff. "But I ain't goin' to quarrel about it. All I'm tellin' you is, if I had the say-so, I'd get these animals to help me catch those robbers. Of course, you're the boss, since you've been put in charge of the case. But you're a city detective. I don't mean nothin' against city detectives, nor against you, personal. I don't know nothin' about you, but you must be a good man or they wouldn't 'a' sent you. But detectin' in the city and detectin' in the country is two different things. I'm a pretty good sheriff in the country, I guess, but in the city I wouldn't be worth much, because I don't know city ways. And you don't know country ways, and that's why I'm tellin' you—"

"Oh, you talk too much," interrupted the detective rudely. "Why don't *you* catch these robbers if you're so smart?"

"Same reason you don't," replied the

sheriff calmly. "I ain't smart enough. Only I'm willin' to say so, and you *ain't*. And I'm willin' to take help where I can get it. If a pig can help me, I call on a pig."

"A pig!" exclaimed the detective. He was so disgusted that he chewed a big piece off the end of his cigar. But he did not say anything more, for at that moment Freddy, who had been listening all the time, decided that he would show himself. He came slowly out of his office, walked over to the fence, and, getting up on his hind legs, leaned his forelegs on the upper rail as a man would have done, and looked inquiringly at the two in the buggy.

The detective gave a gasp of surprise and swallowed his cigar, and although he had chewed up so much of it that it wasn't very big, it hurt quite a lot going down and it was several minutes before he could speak. Then he pointed at Freddy and said hoarsely: "What's that?"

"That's one of 'em," said the sheriff, "the

pig I was tellin' you about." He leaned out of the buggy. "Eh, Freddy? You're a detective, aren't you?" he said.

Freddy nodded solemnly, and the detective gasped again.

"I got a case I'd like your help on," continued the sheriff. "Come on over and sit

under this tree while I tell you about it," and he climbed out of the buggy. When Freddy had got over the fence, they sat down in the grass, while the amazed detective goggled at them for a few moments before himself getting out and joining them.

"You see, it's this way," said the sheriff. "There's been a lot of robberies lately in this neighborhood. Robbers have been breaking in the back windows of banks and stores in nearly all the towns around here and taking all the money. We don't know who they are. So far we haven't got a clue, except that they nearly always wear rubbers, and that they travel in a car with one wobbly rear wheel. It's got so that the people are afraid to leave their places of business now at night, for fear they'll be robbed, and the bankers and business men are most of them sitting up all night with shot-guns and pistols to protect their money. Yes, sir, Freddy, it's getting pretty bad. Because now, you see, the business men are so sleepy in the day-time that when you go in to do business with them, you find them sound asleep behind their counters. There's hardly any business bein' done in Centerboro, on account of the business men being so sleepy.

"That's only one bad thing about it. There's been a lot of accidents through fallin' asleep at the wrong time. Just yesterday my brother fell asleep when he was looking for something to eat in the ice-box, and he lay there with his head on the ice for an hour till we found him, and froze both his ears. Right in the middle of summer—yes, sir! Froze 'em both solid. If you'd 'a' tapped 'em, they'd 'a' broke off like crackers. Course we was careful. We thawed 'em out slow, and they're all right again.

"Then there was old Mr. Winch. He fell asleep driving up Main Street, and his car ran right up on the porch of the Holcomb House and knocked four rocking-chairs to splinters. That wouldn't 'a' been so bad, but Mis' Holcomb was settin' in one of 'em at the time. She was quite upset.

"But that ain't neither here nor there. What I wanted to tell you was that we're at our wits' ends to know what to do. We can't find hide nor hair of these robbers, even though we've got this special detective up from New York. —Oh, I forgot to introduce you to him. Mr. Boner, this is Freddy."

Freddy bowed politely, but the detective frowned. "I ain't going to shake hands with no pig," he growled.

"Suit yourself," said the sheriff, winking at Freddy. "Pig or not, he's shook hands with the President in his time, and that's more than you've done, I bet."

"Oh, come on! Let's get going!" exclaimed Mr. Boner.

"Time enough," replied the sheriff. "Specially as we ain't goin' anywhere in particular." He turned to Freddy. "I just thought," he said, "that maybe, now you've started in as a detective, you'd be willing to give us a hand. I don't know just how you'll go at it, but we're stumped. What do you say?"

"Can he *talk*?" demanded the astonished Mr. Boner.

"Course he can't!" snapped the sheriff. "Who ever heard of a pig that could talk!"

"Well, according to you he can understand everything you're saying," said the detective, not unreasonably.

"That's different," said the sheriff.

While they were wrangling about this, Freddy got up, climbed the fence, and came back presently with the package of one-dollar bills that Cousin Augustus had brought from the trunk in the hermit's house. As soon as they saw it, the two men became very much excited. They examined it carefully, and then the sheriff said to Freddy: "This is from Herbie's Hardware Emporium, that was robbed last month. Gosh, I wish you could talk! Do you know where there's any more of this money?"

Freddy nodded.

"Will you lead us to it?"

But this time Freddy shook his head. Lead them to it indeed, and let them get all the glory of the capture! No, he intended to capture the robbers himself. While they had been talking, he had thought of a plan. It was a good one, too, and he intended to try it out. If he failed, he could call in the sheriff later.

The sheriff was much put out at his refusal. "Oh come, Freddy," he coaxed, "you want to help us, don't you?"

Freddy nodded.

"But you won't show us where the rest of the money is?"

Freddy shook his head again.

"You mean you've got some scheme of your own for getting it back?"

Freddy nodded his head emphatically.

"You see," said the sheriff to Mr. Boner, "he'll help us; but he's going to do it in his own way. And I don't know that I blame him."

"Nonsense!" exclaimed the detective angrily. "Let *me* talk to him." He moved toward the pig, but Freddy was too quick for him and scrambled over the fence. Mr. Boner would have climbed over after him, but the sheriff caught his arm.

"You won't get anywhere that way," he said. "Let him alone. He said he'd help us, and he will. I know these animals."

"You know 'em all right," growled Mr. Boner. "You ought to be livin' in the pen along with 'em. I wash my hands of you. When you're ready to go along, let me know." And he climbed into the buggy and lit a cigar.

"Well, Freddy," said the sheriff, "I guess you'll have to do it your own way. I'll be back along this way day after tomorrow about this time, and if you've got anything for me, you be here. If you want me before that, you know where to find me. And do the best you can. If you can help me catch these rascals, I'll be grateful, you bet; and you know there's five thousand dollars reward offered for their capture. You'll get that, and I'll see that your name is played up big in the newspapers. So long. I'm countin' on you."

As soon as the men had gone, Freddy made his preparations. He got a pencil and paper and drew a plan which you will hear more about later. But to visit the hermit's house he needed a disguise, for he remembered how anxious they had been to catch him when he had been there before. Detectives did much of their work in disguise—workmen's clothes and false whiskers and so on—and Freddy had got together quite a large wardrobe for use in disguising himself, though he had never yet used any of it. Today he picked out a false mustache, a pipe, a cap like Sherlock Holmes's, with a vizor in front and behind and ear-flaps that tied at the top with a tape, and an old suit of Mr. Bean's which was a trifle long in the leg, but otherwise fitted very well.

Walking on his hind legs, with the pipe in his mouth and the cap pulled well down over his eyes, Freddy might have passed for a very small tramp with a very long nose. As there was no looking-glass in his office, he decided to go first up to the house and see what he looked like in Mrs. Bean's mirror. At the same time he would try the effect of his disguise on some of his friends.

To his surprise, he found no animals in the usually busy barnyard. He walked across to the house and rapped on the back door. Mrs. Bean answered. "Good morning," she said politely. "What can I do for you?"

Freddy touched his cap awkwardly and then brushed past her, walked across the kitchen, and started up the back stairs, while Mrs. Bean watched him with amazement and alarm. "See here, young man!" she began—but at that moment Freddy came to grief. By long practice he had learned how to walk on his hind legs, but going upstairs was a different matter. At the fourth step he lost his balance and came tumbling down.

Mrs. Bean stared for a moment, then burst out laughing. "My goodness, Freddy, it's you! For a minute I thought you were a tramp. I suppose you're up to some of your detective tricks again. What won't you animals be doing next!" She picked up his pipe and handed it to him. "Land alive! In that suit you look enough like Mr. Bean to be his brother, except that your legs aren't long enough, and you haven't any beard."

She patted him on the back and went back to her knitting, and Freddy went upstairs on all four legs this time and was soon admiring his get-up in the big mirror in the front

bedroom. As he turned and twisted before the glass, trying the hat and the pipe at different angles, and nodding and bowing to himself with little grunts of satisfaction, he heard a curious sound. He turned quickly. Someone, he thought, had chuckled. But there was no one there, so he went back to

the always pleasant task of admiring himself.

And again came the noise—an unmistak-
able giggle this time.

He stooped and looked under the bed, and
there, not an inch from his nose, was the
grinning face of Jinx, who had been watching him all the time.

It is always embarrassing to find that
someone has been watching you when you
think you are alone, even if you haven't been
doing anything silly; and Freddy knew that
he must have looked very silly in front of the
glass. So he said angrily: "What are you
doing here? Why aren't you watching for
the rats instead of sneaking round and spying on sensible folks?"

To his surprise Jinx, instead of bursting
into his usual loud teasing laugh, came out
from under the bed and said meekly: "Excuse me, Freddy; you did look funny, you
know. But I wasn't spying on you. I was
hiding. They're after me."

"Who are after you?" demanded the pig.

"Haven't you heard?" asked Jinx. "The policemen are after me—Robert and Jock. I tell you, Freddy, I don't know what to do. I wouldn't mind going to jail at any other time. From all I hear, they have a better time inside than we do out. But I *can't* go now—"

"What on earth are you talking about?" interrupted the pig.

"You haven't heard, then," said Jinx. "Well, let me tell you about it—or at least what little I know—for I need your help. You know that for the past few weeks, ever since we got Everett's train back from the rats, I have been spending nearly all my time up in the barn loft, guarding the grain-box. The rats have been trying every way they can to get into it, because, although they say they have got enough grain hidden in their holes under the barn to last all winter, I don't believe they've got very much, and when their supply gives out, they'll have to leave the barn and go back to the woods."

"That'll make old Simon pretty sick," said Freddy.

"Yes, and that's just what I'm working for. He's got to be shown who's boss round here. But if I go to jail, he and his family can just help themselves to all the grain they want. I can't go to jail, Freddy!"

"Well, why should you?" asked the puzzled pig. "You haven't done anything, have you—?"

"Of course I haven't. But just listen to this. This noon I left the barn and went to the house to get my lunch. When I got back, over in the corner of the loft where I usually sit, I saw something that hadn't been there when I left. I went over to look at it, and what do you think was there? Somebody had eaten a crow there and left nothing but his claws and feathers."

"My goodness!" said Freddy.

"Just what I said," went on the cat. "And I was standing there looking at them and trying to figure out how they could have got

there, when in stalks Charles, very haughty
—you know he's never forgiven me for
throwing those tomatoes at him the night he
was elected—and he clears his throat a few
times and then says: 'Ha, it was true, then,
was it?' he says. 'This is a serious matter,
Jinx,' he says. 'This will take some explain-
ing.'

" 'Well,' I said, 'if you can explain it,
Charles, I wish you would. It's beyond me.'

" 'Oh, is it, indeed?' says Charles, very
sarcastic. 'Well, it looks plain enough, Jinx.
Yes, it certainly looks plain enough.'

" 'Oh, cut out the big talk, Charles,' I
said; 'I come back here and find that someone has eaten this crow—'

" 'Someone!' he interrupted. Then he
laughed kind of nastily. '*Some*one! Ha ha,
that's good.'

"He made me so mad that I pretty near
slapped him one. But I kept my temper.
'Look here, Charles,' I said, 'you don't think
I had anything to do with this, do you?

174

Gosh, you ought to know that even an alley cat won't eat a crow.'

" 'They've been known to eat chickens,' he said meaningly. 'But I'm not afraid of you, Jinx. I warn you, it won't be wise for you to try any violence. Jock and Robert are within call. If you dare to so much as lift a paw against me, I have only to call, and they'll be here in a few seconds.'

"Well, Freddy, that kind of pompous talk from Charles, who has always been a good friend of mine, made me pretty wild. If I hadn't seen that there was something serious behind it all, I'd have given him the scare of his life. But I tried to be reasonable. 'Look here, Charles,' I said, 'that kind of talk is just silly. I never even chased a bird of any kind, to say nothing of eating one, and you know it. I found this crow here when I came back from lunch. Now be sensible and tell me what it is all about.'

"Well, then I got it out of him, though he wasn't very friendly about it. It seems that

about the time I was having lunch, one of
the young rats slipped out of the barn, ran
down to the hen-house, and told Charles to
come right away and bring the policemen.
He said I had caught this crow in the barn
and was eating it. Of course Charles came,
and there I was with the crow. Charles must
know perfectly well that I wouldn't do such
a thing, but he's made up his mind to get
even with me about the tomatoes, and so he
wants to send me to jail. So I didn't wait for
Jock and Robert to get there. They were
waiting by the door. I ran down the stairs
and got through the window in Hank's stall,
and I've been hiding here ever since until
I could get a word with you. You've got to
get to the bottom of this for me, Freddy."

"Oh, we can get to the bottom of it all
right," said Freddy. "But it may take some
time. It looks to me as if it was a plot the rats
cooked up to get you sent to jail so they
could have all the grain they wanted."

"Exactly," said the cat. "But what can I

do? I ought to be in the barn, not hiding here under the bed."

"You stay here a little longer," said the pig, "and I'll go down and see if I can pick up any clues."

"But you *do* believe I didn't do it, don't you?" asked Jinx.

"Sure I believe you," said Freddy. "But believing isn't enough to keep you out of jail. We've got to prove it. But you wait; I'll be right back." And struggling out of his disguise, he hurried down the stairs.

In the loft he found a crowd of excited animals, in the middle of which was Charles, who hurried up to the pig as he came in.

177

"Aha, here's the detective!" he cried. "Now we'll get something done. The criminal has escaped, Freddy. You'll have to track him down for us. Spare no pains, in the interests of justice and the safety of this law-abiding barnyard—"

"Oh, shut up, Charles," said the pig good-naturedly. "I know all about it. I don't think for a minute Jinx killed this crow. Clear out, now, all of you. I want to take a look at things."

The animals went reluctantly downstairs, and Freddy looked carefully around. The crow's two claws were laid neatly side by side, and the feathers were in a tidy heap beside them. "Please note," he said to Charles, who, since he was the judge, had been allowed to stay, "that there are no signs of a struggle. If Jinx caught this crow here, the crow would have struggled, and feathers would be strewn all over the place."

"He may have caught it outside," said

Charles. "What difference does that make? All this detective work of yours can't change the fact that he's guilty."

"Maybe they can. Maybe they can," said Freddy musingly. He walked around the pile of feathers, stopping to examine them closely every few steps, then sniffed at them. "Ha!" he said. "Hum! Very curious! Very curious indeed!"

"Very silly, if you ask me," said a harsh voice, as Simon stuck his nose out of a hole in the floor. "You'd be better occupied catching that cat and getting him locked up in jail, than poking round up here, Freddy. He's a friend of yours and all that, but we've got him this time!"

"What do you mean, *you've* got him?" demanded Freddy sharply.

"Oh, nothing," grinned the rat, "except that we all saw him catch the crow and eat him, right in front of our eyes. You can't get round that, I guess."

179

"No, it doesn't look that way, does it?" said Freddy. He picked up a claw and a few feathers and carried them over to the light, where he studied them for a long time. Then he said: "Charles, we'll just keep these things for a while. I'm not at all satisfied that this business is as plain as it looks—not at all satisfied. You can't sentence Jinx to jail until he has had a regular trial. We'll have to get a regular jury together, and all that. I'll leave that to you. But I want to have a few days first to make some inquiries. Let's say we'll have the trial a week from today."

Charles agreed, and the two friends left the loft, followed by Simon's malevolent glare. They took the claws and the feathers along and left them with Robert, who promised to keep them in a safe place. Before he left Charles, Freddy got the rooster to promise that Jinx should be allowed to go free until the day of the trial. "If he's found guilty," the pig said, "you can give him a good long sentence. But until then let's let him go on with his job. He won't run away."

"You talk as if you thought he wasn't guilty," said Charles; "yet the proof's as plain as the nose on your face."

"The nose on my face may be plain or it may not be plain," replied Freddy. "Some think one way and some think different. It's a matter of opinion, Charlie, old boy. And so is this matter of Jinx's guilt. My opinion is, he isn't guilty. But I'm not going to tell you why. You saw as much up there in the barn as I did. If you didn't see what I saw, you'll have to wait until the trial to find out what it was. Good-bye."

Then Freddy went back in the house and upstairs to where Jinx was waiting and told him what had happened. "You just go back to the barn and keep an eye on the rats," he said, "and leave the rest of it to me. I've got another job on my hands right now that will keep me busy for a day or two, but there's plenty of time before your trial to get the evidence I need to prove you didn't eat that crow. Don't you worry."

So Jinx went back to the barn, and Freddy put on his disguise again and set out on his adventure.

CHAPTER X

FREDDY BECOMES A BURGLAR

FREDDY had got such a late start that it was nearly dark in the woods, though above him the tree-tops were bright green and gold in the light of the setting sun. Since he could not swim the creek in his men's clothes, to get to the hermit's house he had to cut through the woods to the bridge and then walk back on the other side. He walked on his hind legs, because after his mishap on the stairs he felt that he needed all the practice he could get if he was to make anybody think he was a man. But the trousers bothered his legs, and he stumbled over roots and tripped over vines and fell into holes until, long before he reached the creek, he was so bruised and hot and out of breath that he sat down on a log to rest. "My goodness," he said to himself, "I'm glad I'm not a man! How they ever manage to do anything or get anywhere in all these clumsy hot clothes I can't imagine! Lords of creation, they call themselves! Humph, I'd rather be a pig any time."

Pretty soon he got up and went on again, and at last he reached the bridge. On the farther side of the bridge a narrow grassy road ran off to the left toward the hermit's house. Freddy followed it. He began to feel rather nervous, but he was a brave pig and he had no thought of turning back.

By this time it was dark. The windows in the hermit's house were lighted up, but they were so dirty that Freddy couldn't see what was going on inside. He could hear music, however—someone was playing the harmonium and a man's voice was singing. The song was "Sweet and Low," but both singer and accompanist were going as fast as they could, and they were never together for more than one note. The singer would be ahead for a time, then the player would put on a burst of speed and pass him, only to get behind again when he stopped to take breath.

Freddy thought this was the funniest singing he had ever heard, and he went up to the front door and peeked through the keyhole, just as the song came to an end. The big man, who was sitting at the harmonium, was wiping sweat from his forehead. "You won that time, Looey," he was saying, "but it's the chords in that second part that slow me up."

"I'll race you on 'Boola Boola,'" said Looey.

'No you won't either," said Red. "You always win on that because you leave out about six 'Boolas,' and I can't keep track

185

when I'm playing. Let's take something where all the words aren't alike. Let's do 'Annie Laurie.' One, two, three—*go*!"

The noise was terrible. If you don't believe it, try singing "Annie Laurie" as fast as you can. Freddy couldn't stand it any longer, and he rapped on the door.

The musicians were going so fast that they couldn't stop for about four bars. Then there was a moment's silence, followed by the clump of heavy shoes, and the door was flung open. Freddy touched his cap and bowed politely.

"My gosh, what's this?" said Red. "Come in, young feller. What can I do for you?"

Freddy stepped inside. The room was lit by three kerosene lamps, but the lamp chimneys were so dirty that they gave very little light, and he felt reasonably sure that if he kept his cap on, they wouldn't know he was a pig. Nevertheless he was scared when they both came close to him and squatted down with their hands on their knees and stared at him.

At first they didn't say anything. They stared at him for a minute, then stood up and stared at each other, then squatted down and stared at him again.

"Well, I'll be jiggered!" said Red.

"So'll I!" said Looey. "He's a—what do you call those little men—a wharf, isn't it?"

"A dwarf," said Red. "You ought to know that, Looey."

"Well, wharf or dwarf, what does it matter what we call him? The point is, what does he call himself? What's your name guy?"

Freddy pointed to his mouth and shook his head.

"He's dumb," said Looey. "What good's a dumb dwarf? Let's throw him out and go on with the music."

Freddy had in his pocket the chart that he had prepared, but although from long practice in handling books and papers he had got so that he could use his forefeet almost as if they were hands, he was afraid that if he took it out and gave it to them they would see that he had hoofs instead of hands, and would realize that he was a pig.

Fortunately at this moment Red said: "Wait! I've got an idea!"

"I hope it's better than the one you had last Thursday," said Looey.

"This is a good one," said Red. "Listen, this dwarf is little, and he's dumb. That means he can get in places where we can't get in, and that he can't tell anybody about it afterwards. How about that back window in the Centerboro National Bank?"

"Gosh!" exclaimed Looey. "That *is* an idea!" He turned to Freddy. "Say, dwarf, would you like to make a lot of money?"

Freddy nodded enthusiastically.

"Fine! You come with us and do just what we tell you to, and we'll give you fifty cents. Come on, Red, get your things on." And almost before he knew what had happened, Freddy was walking back up the dark road with one of the robbers on each side of him.

He hadn't had a chance to show them his chart, and he hadn't the least idea what sort of adventure he was in for now. "Something pretty shady, I bet," he said to himself. "But no use worrying. I'm in with them now, and if I can't catch them after this, I'm a pretty poor detective."

At the bridge they stopped, Red dove into the bushes, and pretty soon there was the sputter of an engine and he drove out into the road in a badly battered open car. Red hoisted Freddy in, and they started off in the direction of Centerboro. Nothing was said on the way. Both the robbers had on rain-coats, black masks, and rubbers and carried pistols in their hands. Looey had hard work driving with the pistol in his hand, and once when he had to shift gears, it went off. It was pointed at the wind-shield when it went off, and Freddy was surprised not to see the glass fly to pieces, but Looey only laughed.

"We don't carry loaded pistols when we're at work," he explained; "it's too easy to have an accident."

As they drove down Main Street, Freddy saw that there were lights in all the stores, just as the sheriff had told him there would be. They slowed up when they came to the bank, and he saw a watchman sitting on the front steps with a gun across his knees. But he paid no attention to them as they turned into the alley next to the bank.

Looey stopped the car in the alley, and they all got out. Red took a step-ladder out of the back seat and put it against the bank wall under a small window. "There you are," he said. "They don't bother to lock this window because it's too small for anybody to get through. But you can get through, and when you're inside, we'll throw this sack in after you, and all you have to do is stuff all the money into the sack, throw it out, and then come out yourself. See?"

Freddy saw all right. He saw that he was going to be a robber in spite of himself, and there was nothing else to do. But he had reckoned without the step-ladder. Climbing the back stairs at the farm with Mr. Bean's trousers on had been bad enough, but this was hopeless. He scrambled up three steps, then caught his left foot in his right trouser leg, stumbled, squealed, and Freddy and the ladder and Looey came down with a crash on the cobble-stones of the alley.

At once the night was full of noise. Windows went up, police whistles blew, men ran out into the streets and began shouting and firing off their guns. Looey scrambled to his feet, tossed Freddy into the car, and climbed in beside him as Red started up the engine. With a roar they dashed out of the alley and up Main Street at full speed. Half a dozen cars swung out into the street behind them as they dodged and twisted to avoid the men who tried to stop them. Red drove magnificently; he almost seemed to dodge the bullets that were fired at them, for none of them hit the car. In less than a minute they were thundering back up the road on which they had come into town, with the pursuit streaming out behind them. In a few minutes more they came to the bridge and crossed it; then Red put on the brakes so quickly that they were all nearly flung through the wind-shield, swung the car round, snapped off the lights, and drove into the bushes where the car had been hidden before.

One by one the pursuing cars flashed past their hiding-place. When the last one had gone by, the two robbers climbed slowly out of the car.

"You can go on back where you came from, dwarf," said Looey in a disgusted voice.

"You ought to be ashamed of yourself," said Red. "Now we haven't got any step-ladder, all on account of you. I was going to put up fresh curtains in the living-room tomorrow, but how I'm to do it without a step-ladder I don't know."

"Go on," said Looey. "Beat it. We don't want anything more to do with you. You haven't got any more sense than a pig."

Freddy grinned to himself in the dark; then he took the paper out of his pocket and handed it to Red.

"What's this?" said the robber. He lit a match to look, then called in an excited voice to his companion: "Look, Looey, he's got a map of that farmer's place—the one that lives across the creek—and it shows where his money is hidden."

They bent over the paper, lighting match after match to examine it. "Map of Mr. Bean's barn, showing location of hidden treasure," it said at the top, and under this Freddy had drawn a chart of the barn, but from one of the box stalls he had drawn a long arrow, at the end of which was written: "Under the floor of this stall is hidden a box containing ten thousand dollars in gold."

The robbers were greatly excited. "This is what he came to give us," said Looey. "Maybe he ain't such a bad dwarf after all." He turned to Freddy. "I'm sorry I said that about your being a pig. Are you sure the money is there?"

Freddy nodded emphatically.

"It's worth trying," said Red. "But, just the same, I ain't taking any chances. We'll take this fellow to the house and tie him up while we go over and see if the money's there. If it is, all right; we'll give him his share. But if it ain't—" He glared at the detective. "Well, he'll regret it, that's all."

This didn't suit Freddy at all, but there was nothing else to be done. They took him back to the hermit's house and tied him in a chair and then set out—on foot, this time, as there would be too many people looking for their automobile on the road.

Freddy was almost in despair. He had made no arrangements for the capture of the robbers. If they went to the barn, they would find nothing in the box stall but a dozen or more animal prisoners. If they came back empty-handed a second time this evening, what would happen to him? To think about it made his clothes feel even more tight and uncomfortable than they already were.

But he didn't think about it long, for the robbers had not been gone more than a minute when there was a movement in a dark corner of the room, and a tiny voice said: "That you, Freddy?"

"Cousin Augustus!" exclaimed Freddy.

"Gosh, I'm glad to hear your voice! Gnaw these ropes through, will you, like a good fellow? I've got to get to the farm before those fellows get there or I'll miss an important capture."

Cousin Augustus's teeth were sharp; in a very few minutes Freddy was free and had thrown off his disguise. "Ha," he exclaimed, "this feels like something! Now I'm equal to anything! But I wonder if I can get there before they do. Tell me, Gus, is there any bird round here that you could wake up and get to take a message to Jock?"

"Sure," said the mouse, "there's a wren lives under the eaves of the porch. I'll just slip up and take a peek in his nest and see if he'll go."

Cousin Augustus wasted no time. In two minutes he was back, accompanied by a very sleepy and rather cross wren, who, however, when he realized that it was Freddy, the renowned detective, who wanted his help, was only too anxious to oblige.

"Fly over and wake up Jock or Robert," said Freddy, "and tell them to clear all the prisoners out of the second box stall right away. Tell 'em they mustn't waste a second. There are two robbers coming over there, and I want them to get into that stall without

any difficulty. Tell Jock to get all the other animals up and have them hide in the barn and keep quiet until the men get in the stall. I'll be there before there's anything else to be done."

The wren repeated the message to be sure he had it straight, and flew off, and then Freddy dashed down to the creek, dove in and swam across, and galloped off through the woods toward the farm. It was much easier going on four feet than it had been on two, and it wasn't long before he reached the pasture. From there on he went more carefully, and by the time he reached the barn he was creeping along like a shadow.

Faint sounds came from the barn, and now and then a light flickered and was gone again. The robbers were there, then! Freddy slipped inside and into Hank's stall. "Hello, Hank," he whispered. "Everything going all right?"

"Far as I know," said Hank. "Though what it all means is beyond me. Just a few minutes ago Jock and Robert and Mrs. Wiggins came in here and made all the prisoners go into one stall, and then they hid —they're over there in the corner—and then two men sneaked in, and it sounds as if they were tearing up the floor. What's it all about anyway?"

But there was no time to explain. Freddy tiptoed across the floor to the door of the stall. Sure enough, there were Red and

Looey, working by the light of an electric torch, heaving at a plank in the floor. With great caution Freddy pushed the heavy door slowly shut and dropped the peg into the hasp.

The robbers heard nothing, and Freddy made no noise, for he had a reason for letting them go on with their work. He went over to the corner where his friends were hiding.

"I guess you can come out now," he said. "We've got 'em safe and fast. This is a great night's work! But what I've been through since I left here you wouldn't believe!"

He started to tell them the tale of his adventures, but suddenly there was a great rattling at the door of the stall. The robbers had found out that they were locked in.

Jock laughed. "Let 'em just try to get out!" he said. "That door will hold an elephant. Anyway I sent down for Peter, in case anything should go wrong. He can handle 'em all right."

199

Freddy started to go on with his story, when they heard a car drive into the yard, and a loud voice shouted: "Hey, farmer! Wake up!"

"I know that voice," said Freddy. "It's the city detective. Well, let's see how many robbers he's caught tonight!"

The animals went to the barn door. A light had sprung up in an upper window, and pretty soon Mr. Bean's head, in its red nightcap with a white tassel, was poked out into the night.

"Stop raisin' all that rumpus, or I'll come down and take my horsewhip to ye!"

"I want to know if you've seen an open car go by here in the past hour," shouted the detective.

"I got something better to do at night than to sit up and watch for open cars," said Mr. Bean. "Now go 'long about your business. I won't have my animals woke up an' disturbed this way."

"I'm huntin' for two robbers in an open car!" shouted Mr. Boner.

"Well, I ain't two robbers in an open car," replied the farmer. "I'm a self-respectin' citizen in a night-shirt, an' what's more, I got a shot-gun in my hand, and if you ain't gone in two minutes—"

Just then another car drove into the yard, and the sheriff got out. Mr. Bean's manner changed as soon as he recognized the newcomer. "Oh, how d'e do, sheriff?" he said. "Who is this feller? Friend of yours?"

The sheriff explained. They were combing the countryside for the two robbers who had been frightened away while trying to rob the Centerboro bank, and they wondered if Mr. Bean had seen or heard anything of them.

"I been in bed for three hours," said the farmer. "But there's Freddy comin' across from the barn. Looks like he might have somethin' to show you. Now I'm goin' back to bed. Look around all you like, but for goodness' sake be quiet about it. I want them animals to get their sleep." And he shut down the window.

Meantime Freddy had come up to the sheriff. He raised a foreleg and waved it toward the barn.

"What is it, Freddy?" asked the sheriff. "You know somethin', I bet."

"Oh, that pig again!" exclaimed the disgusted detective. "Come along, sheriff, there ain't anything here."

"Not so fast," replied the sheriff. "I'm goin' to see." And he followed Freddy to the barn and up to the door of the stall, which was still being shaken by the imprisoned robbers.

"H'm," said the sheriff, lugging out his big pistol. "Looks like you'd caught something this time. Stand aside, animals." And he pulled out the peg.

The door gave way suddenly, and out tumbled Looey and Red.

"Stick up your hands!" said Mr. Boner,

stepping forward. And as the discomfited robbers backed up against the wall with their hands in the air, he turned to the sheriff. "There's your prisoners, sheriff," he said dramatically. "I knew they were here all the time. That's why I stopped in here in the first place."

"Yeah?" said Looey. "Is that so! Well, let me tell you something. It wasn't you that caught us, city detective. You couldn't catch a lame snail."

"No back talk from you!" exclaimed Mr. Boner angrily. "If it wasn't me that caught you, who was it?"

"It was a little feller in a checked cap, if you want to know," said Looey. "And if all you detectives was as smart as him, you'd have caught us long ago."

"Here's your 'little feller,'" said the sheriff, pushing Freddy forward.

"There you go with your pig again," snorted the disgusted Boner. "I drove into this barnyard to look for 'em, didn't I? And they're here, ain't they? Well, then, who caught 'em? And who's going to believe that a pig could have done it?"

"The pig done it," said the sheriff doggedly, "and the pig ought to get the credit, *and* the reward!"

Looey and Red were staring at Freddy in amazement. "A pig!" exclaimed Red. "My gosh, Looey, a *pig!*"

"Pig, all right," replied Looey wearily. "Gee, we're a hot pair of robbers. Caught by a pig!" And then as Mr. Boner started in again to argue that it was he that should get the reward, Looey added: "Well, take us away and lock us up. Anywhere where we won't have to listen to this guy talk any more."

Mr. Bean, in his long white night-shirt and carrying a lantern, had appeared a few moments earlier in the barn door. "Trying to take the credit from my animals, is he?" he muttered. "We'll soon fix that." And he put his head outside and called softly:

"Peter! Get rid of this fellow for us, will you?"

"And I want to tell *you* something too, Mr. Sheriff," Mr. Boner was saying. "You ain't done anything on this case, any more than your friend the pig has, and I'm going to give my own story of the capture to the

newspapers, and don't you try to stop me. They're going to say that Mr. Montague Boner, the famous detective, was successful in putting an end to the depredations in upstate banking circles last night. With his brilliant capture of the two—"

Here he stopped, and abruptly, for something rough and furry had rubbed up against him. He turned to look. Peter, the bear, was standing on his hind legs beside him, his mouth wide open, his arms spread out, looking twice his size in the flickering lantern-light.

Mr. Boner opened his mouth almost as wide as Peter's, and out of it came a long yell. Then he dashed for the door. He yelled as he reached the yard, and he continued to yell as he turned out of the gate and dashed off up the road, with Peter loping along easily a few feet behind him. The animals crowded to the door; they could see nothing, but they could hear those diminishing yells dying away in the direction of Centerboro, until at last through the calm night they came back as a thin thread of sound, like the whine of a mosquito. And presently that was gone too, and there was silence.

"Thank you, Mr. Bean, and animals all," said the sheriff. "I'll be getting along now. I'll be up in the morning, Freddy, to have you show me where all that stolen money is.

I'll bring the reward with me. Come along, you two. Couple o' nice cells all made up for you, with clean towels and flowers in the vases and everything. Night, all."

Mr. Bean said good night; then he turned to the animals. "Now don't sit up talking half the night," he said gruffly. "Lots of time to go over it all tomorrow. I'm proud of you, Freddy." He patted the pig clumsily on the shoulder. "Good night." And he stumped off toward the house.

"Well," said Mrs. Wiggins with a deep sigh, "*this* has been a night, I *must* say. But Mr. Bean is right; we must get off to bed. Only I want to hear all about it first thing in the morning."

The animals dispersed slowly. But Freddy drew Jinx aside, and as soon as the others were gone, "Look here, Jinx," he said, "the boards those robbers pulled up in that stall are just about over where the rats store their grain. Better have a look at that before you turn in, eh?"

Jinx twitched his whiskers twice, clapped Freddy on the back with a paw, then winked broadly, and as the pig left the barn, he glanced back and saw Jinx creep like a shadow through the open door of the box stall.

CHAPTER XI

THE TRIAL

AT last came the day of the trial. From early morning the roads and field paths were full of animals, streaming toward the cow-barn, where Jinx was to be tried for the murder and subsequent eating of the crow. Many of them had brought their lunch with them, for there was no question that the trial would be a long and hard-fought legal battle. The general opinion through the countryside was that the cat was guilty, but Jinx's friends had stuck by him loyally, even in face of what seemed almost certain guilt. "For," said they, "we stand on Jinx's past record, as well as on the general nature of cats. Jinx has never been known to chase, much less to eat, even a sparrow. And it is a well-known fact that no cat will eat a crow. We don't care what the rats say. We believe him innocent."

The trial was set for two o'clock. From the door of his office Freddy, in the intervals of his work, could see the animals streaming by. But he was very busy that morning. The capture of the robbers had made a great impression, and accounts of it had been published in every paper in the country. The day before, a deputation of Centerboro citizens, headed by the mayor in a silk hat, had come to tender him their official thanks and to pay him the reward of five thousand dollars. After the ceremony, which included speeches by several prominent bankers and business men, a number of the deputation had stayed behind to engage his services in various matters which they wanted cleared up. Many animals, too, from distant villages, who had

now heard for the first time of his remark-
able ability as a detective, had brought him
their troubles, so that he had work enough
to keep him busy for a year or more. He listened to them all with courteous attention,
giving as much of his time and interest to
the cousin of Henrietta's from whom a china

egg had been stolen as to the wealthy banker
from Green's Corners who wanted assistance in finding his long-lost daughter.

He sat inside the shed, listening gravely
to his clients, exchanging now and then a
word with his partner, Mrs. Wiggins—who
had to sit outside the door because there was
not room for her inside—giving orders to

his subordinates, the mice and squirrels and other small animals to whom were given the less important tasks of detecting, and receiving the reports of other birds and animals who hurried in and out on his errands. Beside him the money he had received as a reward was piled up in plain sight—"for no one," said Freddy, "would dare to steal it now. They know that if they tried it, we'd catch 'em and have 'em clapped in jail within twenty-four hours."

Pretty soon Jinx himself came along. He sat down and waited until Freddy had finished with another client, then went in and said good morning.

"Good morning, Jinx," said Freddy. "How's everything up at the house?"

"Oh, all right, I guess," replied the cat. "But I tell you, Freddy, I'm a little nervous, and that's a fact. Are you *sure* you can get me off? As I told you, I wouldn't mind so much going to jail at any other time, but right now it's as much as my job's worth not to be where I can keep those rats in their place."

"I thought you'd got the upper hand of them since the other night," said Freddy.

"So I have. I captured Ezra and two of Simon's nephews and locked them up; and where those boards were ripped up, I found nearly a bushel of grain, which the mice carried back to the grain-box while I stood guard, but Simon is still there, and this morning, while Mr. Bean was getting the boards ready to be put back in place and nailed down, Simon stuck his head out of his hole and gave me the laugh. 'You'll never drive us out of the barn, Jinx,' he said. 'I admit you got most of our supplies, but by this time tomorrow night,' he said, 'you'll be locked up safe and tight, and then, boy! Won't we have a feast! And by the time you get out,' he said, 'we'll have enough more stored away so you'll never get us out.' "

"Well, as I've told you before," said Freddy, "you aren't going to be locked up.

I've got this case just where I want it, and the trial will prove some things about those rats that will surprise you. It isn't just what I believe—it's what I can *prove*. And I can prove you didn't kill any crow."

"Well," said the cat, "I wish you'd tell me—"

"No," interrupted the pig, "I'm not going to tell you anything. It's a long story and you'll hear it all in court. There isn't time for it now. Just be patient, and don't worry, and everything'll come out all right, I promise you."

"I hope you're right," said Jinx with a sigh. "Oh, gosh!" he exclaimed suddenly, glancing out of the door, "here's Charles. I'm off, Freddy. I'll lose my temper if I talk to that big stuffed shirt, and goodness only knows what might happen then."

"Yes, you'd better go along," said Freddy. "See you in court.—Morning, Charles, how's everything in the hen-house this morning?" he said as the rooster, with an indignant glance at the departing cat, entered the office.

"Everything is all right, thank you," said Charles stiffly. "I must say, Freddy, I can't approve of your hob-nobbing with criminals this way."

"Oh, hob-nobbing with your grandmother's tail-feathers!" exclaimed the pig good-naturedly. "Don't try that high and mighty stuff with me, that's known you since you were a little woolly chicken that couldn't say anything but 'Peep, peep,' like a treetoad!"

"That's all very well, Freddy," said the rooster, "but, fond as I have been of Jinx in the past, it is my belief that by committing this crime he has forfeited the friendship and esteem of all decent animals, and I cannot—"

"Oh, save the speech till later in the day," interrupted Freddy. "But just let me tell you this: Jinx is innocent, and I can prove it, and I'm going to prove it this afternoon, and you're going to feel very silly when you know the truth and remember all the things you've said about him. And now let's talk of something else. I've been wanting to see you to ask you what you thought about conditions in the jail. It isn't as overcrowded as it was before we threw out all the animals who hadn't been sentenced at all, but it seems to me that we could make it a little less like a club if you pardoned any animals who seemed to be having too good a time there, and put them out. I think that if the animals knew that they weren't going to be allowed just to stay there and enjoy themselves, they wouldn't be so anxious to get in, and there wouldn't be so many of them stealing things just so they'd be put there."

"An excellent idea, Freddy," said the judge. "And I'd like to start with that Eric. You know what he's done? He's been making speeches to the other prisoners, telling them how silly they are to want to stay out of jail when they can have so much better fun inside, and he's organized a lot of them into a club called the Hoho Club. To join it you have to give your word that as soon as your sentence is up and you're free again, you will commit some crime so you'll be put right back in."

"What does 'Hoho' mean?" asked Mrs. Wiggins.

"Hilarious Order of Habitual Offenders," said Charles.

"Which leaves me right where I was before," said Mrs. Wiggins. "What does *that* mean?"

"An habitual offender," explained Freddy,

"is an animal who makes a habit of committing offenses, so he'll go to jail."

"Oh!" said Mrs. Wiggins.

"They've even got a song they sing," said
Charles angrily. "It goes something like
this:

> Habitually we offend
>   Against our country's laws.
> It works out better in the end
>   Than being good, because —
>
> No home has a superior
>   Or cheerier interior
> Than this old jail,
> The which we hail
>   With constant loud applause,
>
> For—
>
> Be it ever so crowded
>   There's no—o place like jail!"

"It's not a very good song," said Freddy.
"Or perhaps it's the way you sing it."

"Not enough expression," put in Mrs.
Wiggins.

"Oh, who asked you to criticize my singing?" asked Charles crossly. "I was just telling you—"

"Sure, sure," said Freddy soothingly, "we agree with you. Something's got to be done. But wait till after the trial this afternoon. I've got an idea how we can fix this Hoho Club so they won't be so anxious to come up before the judge. I'll see you then, Charles."

"Everything is in now except Eeny's report, isn't it?" asked Mrs. Wiggins, as soon as Charles had gone.

"Yes," said Freddy, "and he'll meet me at the court-room. I suppose we'd better be getting on over and see that all our witnesses are there. Here's the evidence." He dragged out a market basket in which were the claws and feathers that had been found in the loft, along with several other small objects, and Mrs. Wiggins hooked it up with her horn and they started off.

The cow-barn was full, and a big mob of animals who could not find room inside were crowded about the door. Mrs. Wiggins pushed her way good-naturedly through the crowd, and Freddy followed. "What you got in the basket?" called a horse. "You going to use it to carry out what's left of Jinx after the trial?"

The crowd laughed, and Freddy turned around. "Listen, horse," he said, "we've got the proofs of Jinx's innocence in this basket, and what do you say to that?"

"Why, I say I hope it's true," replied the horse, and the other animals raised a cheer.

At the far end of the barn was an old phaeton, which the animals had brought back from Florida two years before, and on the front seat stood Charles, very dignified and grand, only occasionally exchanging a few words in an undertone with Peter, the bear, who was foreman of the jury. Charles had selected the twelve members of the jury, and they sat in a double row to the left of the phaeton: Peter and Mrs. Wogus and Hank and Bill, the goat, and two sheep in the back row, and in the front row, because they were smaller, Cecil, the porcupine, and Emma's Uncle Wesley, and two mice, Quik and Eek, and Freddy's sister's husband, Archie, who was so fat that he snored, even when he was wide awake. The twelfth jury-man, Mr. Webb, the spider, had spun a thread down from the roof and hung there, just above the rest of the jury, where he could see and hear everything, but wouldn't be in danger of being stepped on. In the back seat of the phaeton was the prisoner, Jinx, looking much worried.

Every available inch of space in the barn was occupied. Window-sills, beams, and rafters were lined with field mice, chip-munks, squirrels, and birds, and the pressure of the crowd on the floor was so great that even before the trial began, several smaller animals fainted and had to be carried out. Just in front of the judge a space had been kept clear, and as Freddy moved up to one side of this, Eeny darted out from under the phaeton.

"I found it at last, Freddy," he said. "They didn't get it from Mr. Bean's house at all. It was Miss McMinnickle's. Something Prinny said put me on to it, and I went down there and got in the house, and, sure enough, they'd tipped it over on her writing-desk and spilled a lot, and you could see their footprints on the blotter."

"Fine!" said Freddy. "That's great work, Eeny!"

"I brought a piece of the blotting-paper along," said the mouse. "Jock has it for safe keeping."

"Good. Now stick round. I'll need your testimony before very long. Believe me, we're going to give those rats a surprise!"

"Order in the court!" called Charles in his most important voice. "Silence, please. Now, gentlemen of the jury—"

"Ladies, too," whispered Jock, pointing toward Mrs. Wogus.

"You can't say 'ladies' when there's only one," snapped Charles.

"Well, you've got to say *something*, you can't just leave her out entirely."

"Lady and gentlemen of the jury," said Charles, "you are here to decide from the evidence presented to you at this time upon the guilt or innocence of one, Jinx, a cat in the employ of Mr. Bean, who is charged with the murder, and subsequent eating, of an unknown crow, in the barn on August 7 last. Ferdinand, as a member of the great crow family, will conduct the prosecution. Frederick, the well-known detective, will conduct the defense, with the assistance of his colleague, Mrs. Wiggins. Mr. Ferdinand, will you call your witnesses?"

Ferdinand hopped up to the dash-board of the buggy, cleared his throat with a harsh caw, fixed the foreman of the jury with his sardonic eye, and said:

"As you doubtless know, ladies and gentlemen, the chief witnesses for the prosecution are Simon and his family, a band of rats who are living illegally, and without permission from Mr. Bean, in the barn. This in itself constitutes a misdemeanor which may well in time bring them as prisoners into this court. Nevertheless, their crimes and offenses have nothing to do with the case

which we are now considering, and I wish you, in listening to their evidence, to make up your opinion without reference to any prejudice you may have against them on that score. It is Jinx who is being tried now, not the rats. Do I make myself clear?"

Mrs. Wogus spoke up. "No," she said bluntly, "you don't."

"I will try to make myself more clear,"

said the crow. "You believe these rats are thieves, don't you?"

"Yes," said the cow, "I certainly do."

"Probably a good many of us here agree with you," said Ferdinand. "Still, they have a story to tell of what they saw, and in judging of the truth of that story you must not be influenced by that belief. In other words, just because you think they are thieves, you mustn't also think they are liars."

"But I do," said Mrs. Wogus. "How can I help it?"

"Because it hasn't anything to do with *this* case," said Charles.

"Certainly it has," said the cow.

"You'd better get on with your case," said Charles to Ferdinand, and the crow, seeing that he was only throwing doubts on the truthfulness of his witnesses by continuing his efforts to explain, nodded his head.

"Well," he said, "I can only ask you to judge by the evidence that will be presented to you. I may say that the rats were reluctant to come here and testify, since it meant leaving their homes under the barn, where they feel themselves safe. In order to get them here at all I have had to get a promise from the judge that they shall not be molested until the trial is over. I will now call my first witness, Simon."

The old gray rat crept out from under the buggy, where he and his family had been waiting, and took his place in the open space reserved for witnesses.

"Tell the jury in your own words what you saw," said Ferdinand.

Simon's whiskers twitched and his eyes slid round toward Jinx, who was crouched in the back seat of the buggy, his tail moving gently from side to side. "I'd like to have your word, your honor," he said to Charles, "that my children and I will be allowed to give our evidence and go back home without being assaulted. I'm a poor rat, and I ain't done harm to anybody. We rats have to live.

That's something that you animals don't ever seem to think of—"

"Silence!" said Charles sternly. "We're not trying *your* case now."

"No, sir," said Simon humbly. "But if you'd just give your word—"

"The judge and the jury and all the animals, including myself and the prisoner," put in Freddy, "have agreed that until the trial is over, no harm shall come to you. Am I right, Your Honor?"

"That was the agreement," said Charles.

"Yes," said Simon, "but will you give me safe conduct back to the barn after the trial?"

Charles was about to speak, but Freddy interrupted him. "Unless you commit some crime between now and the time the trial is over," he said, "you'll be allowed to go back with your family."

This seemed to satisfy Simon, who, with an uneasy eye on Jinx, began to tell his story.

"At noon on August 7, I and my family were peacefully eating our dinner when we heard a great commotion in the loft. We rushed up through our secret passageways in the walls and, looking out from our holes, saw one of the most terrible sights we have ever witnessed. This cat, who now stands before the bar of justice—this wicked felon, whose vile sins have at last found him out—this evil—"

"Come, come, Simon," interrupted Freddy, "get on with your story, and don't call names."

"Ah, forgive me, Your Honor," said Simon, with a hypocritical leer at Charles,

228

"for letting my feelings get the best of me. It is my hatred and loathing for such detestable crimes that has led me into saying more than I intended—"

"And if you say much more like that," put in Jinx with an angry swish of his tail, "there'll be a *real* murder to investigate in about two seconds. One good overhand swipe at you, you oily old rodent, and there'll be one less at breakfast tomorrow morning under the barn!"

"Order!" shouted Charles. "Continue with your story, rat, and keep your opinions to yourself."

"Yes, Your Honor," said Simon with mock humility. "As I was saying, this—this cat had pounced upon a poor, inoffensive little crow and, when we had reached a point from which we could see what was going on, was tearing him limb from limb with unparalleled ferocity. We shouted, Your Honor; we called upon him to stop; but he merely grinned wildly and went on with his butchery. I sent one of my grandchildren to notify the police at once, but then there was nothing for us to do but watch until the horrid deed was done. We wept, Your Honor— I will not conceal it from you that in our horror and indignation, in our helplessness and in our sorrow for the fate of this wretched bird, we wept bitter tears. But they were as unavailing as our threats and warnings. The cruel and relentless animal was—" Simon stopped suddenly as Jinx leaped to his feet. "That, Your Honor," he said hastily, "is my story."

Following Simon came eight other rats who testified to having seen the same thing; then Charles took the stand and told of having been summoned to the barn, where he found Jinx, evidently terrified at having been discovered in his crime. Then, Freddy having said that he would like to cross-examine Simon, the rat again came forward.

"How large are the rat-holes that lead into the loft?" asked the pig.

"You've seen 'em; you ought to know," replied the rat with a grin.

"That's not what I asked you," snapped Freddy. "Are they big enough for a cat to get through?"

"No cat ever got through 'em."

"Just about big enough for one rat, then?"

"Just about."

"And how many are there?"

"Three," said Simon. "There ain't any harm in my telling you that."

"Oh, isn't there?" said Freddy. "Well, will you tell me how nine rats, with only three holes big enough for one rat each, managed to see everything that went on?"

Simon snarled and twitched his whiskers. "Trying to make me out a liar, are you?" he demanded. "Well, let me tell you, smarty that three rats can see out of one rat-hole all right."

"How do they stand when they're looking out?" asked Freddy. "They can't stand beside each other, and if they stand one behind the other, how can they see?"

"How do I know how they do it!" snarled Simon. "They did it all right, didn't they? You heard 'em say they saw it, didn't you?"

"Sure, I heard 'em," said Freddy pleasantly, and, turning to Charles: "That's all, Your Honor," he said.

Simon retreated under the buggy, where a chatter and squeaking of excited rat voices could be heard, while the jury examined the claws and feathers of the crow. Evidently Freddy's questions had disturbed the witnesses somewhat, but they quieted down when Freddy announced that if the prosecution had no other evidence to present, he would like to call a few witnesses in the defense.

The first was Ferdinand himself, who testified that he did not know who the dead crow could be. So far as he knew, no crows had been reported missing within a day's flight in any direction from the farm.

"At this time of year crows are not likely to fly more than a day's flight in any direction, are they?" asked Freddy.

"No," said Ferdinand. "But this crow might have been going on a visit to relatives in another district. It is probable that this was the case."

"Crows don't usually make such visits, do they?"

"No."

"Have you ever known of a crow doing it?"

"No," said Ferdinand, "but that's no reason why one might not do it."

"True," said Freddy, "but I would say that it is *possible*, rather than probable, wouldn't you?"

"Why, yes, perhaps," said Ferdinand unwillingly.

"Thank you, that's all," said Freddy. "I will now call Eeny."

The mouse took the stand and told how he had been sent by Freddy to inspect the writing-desks of all the neighbors within half a mile of the farm. At none of them had he found anything unusual or out of the way until he had visited Miss McMinnickle's house. Here he had found signs that the ink-bottle had recently been overturned, and although Miss McMinnickle had evidently sopped up the ink and washed and cleaned the desk, the blotter on which the bottle had been standing showed several large blots, and the inky prints of many small feet. He had brought away with him a piece of this blotter, which Freddy presented to the jury for their inspection.

Freddy then called Prinny, Miss McMinnickle's dog, who testified that on August 5 Miss McMinnickle had had chicken for supper. Charles shuddered at this, and his daughter Leah, who was perched on a beam over the jury-box, fainted dead away and fell with a thump to the floor. When she had been carried outside and order had been restored, Freddy said:

"When did you last see the claws of this chicken?"

"I object!" exclaimed Ferdinand, before Prinny could answer. "Your Honor, the question of what this Miss McMinnickle had for supper on the day before this brutal murder has nothing to do—"

"And *I* object, Your Honor," shouted Freddy suddenly. "It is not yet proved that any murder has been committed, and I submit that Ferdinand is endeavoring to prejudice the jury."

"Order in the court!" crowed Charles, as the animals surged closer so as not to miss a word of this clash between the opposing counsel. "You *can't* both object at the same time! What did you object to, Ferdinand?"

The crow repeated his remark.

"I intend to show, Your Honor," said Freddy, "that the question of what this lady had for supper has a very close bearing on the case. May I proceed?"

"Proceed," said the judge, who was somewhat flustered and couldn't think of anything else to say.

Freddy repeated his question, and Prinny said: "I last saw them on the rubbish heap on the morning of August 6."

"And did you visit the rubbish pile later on the same day?"

"I did."

"And they were there?"

"No," said Prinny, "they had disappeared."

Ferdinand did not cross-examine this witness, and Freddy then called Simon's son Zeke. There was a flutter of interest as Zeke took the stand, and the animals pushed forward until Charles threatened to have the court-room cleared unless they were quiet. Even Archie opened his little eyes, which had been tight shut for some time, and stopped snoring.

"Now, Zeke," said Freddy, "I suppose you are anxious to answer all the questions I ask you fully and truthfully?"

"Oh yes, sir," said Zeke, opening his eyes wide and trying to look truthful, but only succeeding in looking as if he had a stomach-ache.

"Very well," said Freddy. He paused a moment, then suddenly he glared at the rat. "Where were you on the morning of August 6?" he shouted.

Zeke looked startled. "Why, sir, I—I was at—home all day. Yes, sir, at home."

"You were, eh?" roared Freddy. "And what if I tell you that I have witnesses to prove that you were *not* home?"

"Why, I might have been out for a little

237

while, sir. I can't exactly remember. I do go out once in a while."

"You *were* out, then?"

"Yes, sir. I—I may have been."

"Good," said Freddy. "Now cast your mind back to the morning of August 6. You were out taking a walk, let us say. You went up along the side of the road to Miss Mc-Minnickle's house. Am I right so far?"

"Why, honestly, sir, I can't remember. I was just out getting a little air. I might have gone up that way. I—"

"You *might* have gone that way?" said Freddy. "I suggest that you went directly to Miss McMinnickle's house, to which you gained entrance through a cellar window. You then went upstairs and got up on the kitchen table and ate part of a ham—"

"Oh no, sir!" exclaimed the rat. "I wasn't in the kitchen at all. I—"

"Shut up, you fool!" came Simon's snarling voice from under the buggy, and immediately Ferdinand began fluttering his wings

238

and shouting: "Stop! Stop! I object! Your Honor, I object on two counts. First, Zeke's whereabouts on the day before the mur—I should say, the alleged crime—have nothing to do with this case. Second, Freddy is trying to intimidate this witness."

"Objections not sustained," snapped Charles. "Even if this rat's whereabouts have nothing to do with the case, I guess everybody here wants to know what he was doing at Miss McMinnickle's. And, second, if anything can be done by Freddy or any other animal to intimidate him, I want to see it done. Proceed, Freddy."

"Oh, shucks!" exclaimed Ferdinand disgustedly. "That isn't any way to try a case, Charles. Use a little sense, will you?"

"If you don't like the way this case is being tried, crow," said Charles with dignity, "you are at liberty to leave. This court will not be dictated to. I'm here to sentence Jinx, and sentence him I will, but I shall do it in my own way."

"Perfectly satisfactory to me, Your Honor," said Ferdinand.

"But it's not to me," said Freddy. "You are *not* here to sentence Jinx, Charles; you're here to see that justice is done."

"Well, justice is done if I sentence him, isn't it?" demanded the rooster.

"Not if he's innocent."

"But he isn't innocent," exclaimed Charles. "Everybody knows that."

"No free-born American animal," said Freddy, "can be convicted of a crime until he is proved guilty. I appeal to the audience in this court-room. What should we do with a judge who condemns a prisoner before he has stood trial?"

"Depose him! Throw him out! Elect another judge!" shouted the animals.

"Order in the court!" screamed Charles. "My duty here is to give judgment—"

"You can't give what you haven't got!" called a voice. "You never had any judgment, Charles, and you know it!"

There was a shout of laughter, but Freddy stood up on his hind legs and motioned for silence, and the noise quieted down.

"I'm sure," he said, "that our worthy judge spoke without thinking. He knows as well as you do that a prisoner is considered innocent until he is proved guilty. I merely wished to call attention to the fact that he is letting his dislike of Jinx interfere with his sense of justice. You see that, don't you, Charles?"

"Oh, I suppose so," replied the harassed rooster. "Get on with your trial, will you, and quit picking on *me*."

"Very well," said Freddy. "Now, Zeke, by your own admission, you were in Miss McMinnickle's house on the morning of the 6th. Will you tell us what you did there?"

"You don't have to answer that," called Simon from under the buggy. "You don't have to answer any question if you feel that the answer would tend to incriminate or degrade you."

"All right, I won't answer that," said Zeke.

"You feel that the answer would incriminate or degrade you?" asked Freddy.

"Yes. A lot."

"Good," said Freddy. "Consider yourself incriminated and degraded, then. Ferdinand, do you wish to cross-examine this degraded witness?"

"No," said Ferdinand crossly. "He hasn't anything to do with this case. I've said that all along."

So Freddy called two more witnesses. The first, a squirrel, testified to having seen a rat carrying a bird's claw of some kind going toward the barn on the morning of the 6th. The second, a blue jay, testified that on the same day he had come home to his nest unexpectedly and had found two rats looking into it. He had flown at them and driven them away and had then looked about carefully, but could find nothing missing except a number of long feathers which had formed part of the lining of the nest. Later in the day he had seen two rats, who might or might not have been the same two, running through the woods carrying in their mouths a number of feathers of different kinds. They had evidently been gathering them for some purpose of their own.

The crowd, which could not see what all this had to do with the case and had been getting restless, became quiet again when Freddy announced that he would call no more witnesses, but would sum up his case for the jury.

CHAPTER XII
FREDDY SUMS UP

"I WILL show you, gentlemen of the jury," said Freddy, "not only that Jinx is innocent of this crime, but that no crime has been committed. I will show you further that certain animals have been guilty of a conspiracy to deprive Jinx of his liberty and to cause him to be sentenced for this non-existent crime.

"Now may I ask you to examine carefully the claws and feathers which are alleged to be those of a crow, killed and eaten by Jinx. You will remember that two chicken claws disappeared from Miss McMinnickle's rubbish heap on the 6th, and that, by his own admission, Zeke was near that house at the same time. I suggest to you that those claws you have there are not crow's claws at all, but the chicken's claws, which were taken by Zeke or one of his relatives and placed in the barn."

"But these claws are black," said Peter.

"True," said Freddy. "They have been colored black with ink. They were taken into the house by the rats who tipped over the ink-bottle on Miss McMinnickle's desk while they were dyeing the claws. Here is a portion of the blotter taken from that desk. You will see on it the plain prints of rats' feet.

"Furthermore, you have heard evidence to the effect that several rats were gathering feathers of various kinds in the woods on the 6th. Now please examine carefully the alleged crow's feathers. I think you will find that they are of very different kinds. They are all black, true; but if you will smell of them and then smell of the ink-soaked blotter, you will find the two smells exactly the same. They smell, in fact, of ink. They have been dyed, just as the claws were dyed."

Some confusion was caused by the efforts of the jury to smell of the feathers, which are very difficult things to smell of without getting your nose tickled. There was a tremendous outburst of sneezing in the jury-box, in the course of which the feathers were scattered all about the court-room, but when it was over and the feathers had been gathered together again, it was plain that the jury had accepted Freddy's theory.

"I will ask you now," went on the pig, "to remember several facts. There was no sign of a struggle in the barn, as there would have been if Jinx had actually caught a crow and eaten him there. The claws and feathers were laid out in a neat pile. Again, although there was only room in the three rat-holes for three rats to see what was going on in the loft, nine rats testified to having seen

Jinx catch and eat the crow. Lastly, no crow is known to be missing, although, as all of you know, if one crow so much as loses a tail-feather, you will hear the crows cawing and shouting and complaining about it for weeks afterwards.

"Now, what happened was this, as you probably all see by this time. The rats wanted to get Jinx out of the way, so they could get a fresh supply of grain from the grain-box in the loft. They got the feathers and claws as I have shown you, dyed them black with ink, put them out on the floor, and then when Jinx came in, accused him of the crime. There is not a word of truth in their evidence. It is one of the most dastardly attempts to defeat the ends of justice which have ever come under my notice. I leave the case with you, confident that your verdict will free the prisoner."

There was much shouting and cheering as Freddy concluded, and then Ferdinand rose to make his speech to the jury. He knew that he had a weak case, so he said very little about the facts. His attack was rather upon Freddy than upon the evidence that had been collected.

"A very clever theory our distinguished colleague and eminent detective has presented to us," he said. "A little too clever, it seems to me. After all, it is the business of a detective to construct theories. But what we are concerned with here is the truth. We are plain animals; we like things plain and simple. Here is a dead bird, and beside it a cat. What is plainer than that? Do we need all this talk of ink and blue jays and chicken suppers to convince us of something that gives the lie to what is in front of our very noses? I think not. I think we all agree that two and two make four. I think we prefer such a statement as that to a long explanation why two and two should make six. With all due respect and admiration for the brilliance of the theory which Freddy has presented to us, I do not see how your verdict can be other than 'Guilty.'"

There was some cheering at the end of Ferdinand's speech, but it was more for the cleverness with which he had avoided the facts than because the audience agreed with him. And then Charles got up to speak. His speech was perhaps the best of the three. He referred to the grave responsibility which rested on the members of the jury, to the great care which they must exercise in deciding on the guilt or innocence of the prisoner. They must not be swayed by prejudice, he said, but must look at the facts as facts, must remember that— But it was a very long speech and, though beautifully worded, meant very little, so I will not give it in full. If you are interested in reading it, it will be possible to get a copy, for Freddy later wrote out an account of the trial on his typewriter, with all the speeches in full, which is kept with other documents in the

Bean Archives, neatly labeled "The State vs. Jinx," where I have seen it myself.

The jury whispered together for a few minutes while the audience waited breathlessly for the verdict, and Jinx sat quite still, looking rather worried, but with one eye on the dark space under the buggy where the rats were chattering together. Then Peter got up.

"Your Honor, our verdict is ready," he said.

"What is it?" asked Charles.

"Not guilty!" said Peter.

At the words there was a burst of cheering that shook the barn and knocked two chipmunks off the beam where they had been sitting. Mr. Webb ran hastily up his thread and watched the rest of the proceedings from the roof. Jinx had jumped down from the buggy to receive the congratulations of his friends, who were crowding round him. But Freddy spoke to Charles, who crowed at the top of his lungs for order, and presently there was quiet.

"Ladies and gentlemen," said the detective, "there is another matter before this court before it adjourns. I call for the arrest of Simon and his family on the charge of conspiracy, perjury, and just plain lying."

The squeaking and chattering under the buggy became louder, and Ferdinand said: "You can't do that, Freddy. We promised 'em they could go back to the barn in safety."

"If you remember what I said," replied the pig, "it was that unless they had committed some fresh crime before the trial was over, they might go back in safety. But they *have* committed a fresh crime. They didn't tell the truth about Jinx, and that's a crime, isn't it?"

"H'm," said Ferdinand, "I guess it is. Simon, come out here."

Simon was no coward; he could fight when he had to. He came out now, grinning wickedly. He knew better than to argue however. "You're all against me," he said. "Fat pig and stupid cow and silly sheep and stuffed-shirt rooster and all of you. Well, go ahead; sentence us to jail and see if we care. That's all you can do. Come on out, Zeke, and the rest of you."

The other rats were not so anxious to come out, but they were more afraid of Simon than of any of the other animals except the cat, so presently they crept out into the open space beside their leader.

"We'll have this trial in order," said Charles. "We've got a jury here, and you can pick somebody to defend you."

"I'll take care of my own case," snarled Simon.

"All right. Jinx, you see that none of them try to get away."

"Yeah!" said Jinx. "Watch me!" And he walked up and sat down beside Simon, who bared his teeth. But Jinx, who was a good natured cat and couldn't bear a grudge for

very long, even when he had such good reason for it as he now had, merely winked at
the rat. "Be yourself, Simon," he said.

One by one the rats were questioned, their
names and ages taken, and the question put
to them whether they had any reason to give
why they shouldn't be sentenced. Acting under Simon's instructions, they all said no.
The smallest of the rats caused some amuse-
ment when he gave his name as Olfred.

"There isn't any such name!" said
Charles.

"There is too!" exclaimed the rat. "I've
got it, haven't I?"

"How do you spell it?" asked the rooster.

"O-l-f-r-e-d," said the rat.

"It ought to be spelled with an A," said
Charles. "Alfred—that's what it is."

"It isn't either. It's Olfred," insisted the
rat.

"Nonsense!" exclaimed the judge sharply.
"Don't you suppose I know?"

"No, you don't. Just because you never

heard of it don't mean anything. There's lots of names you never heard of."

"Is that so!" exclaimed Charles angrily. "I bet you can't tell me one that I don't know."

"Yes I can," said Olfred. "There's Egwin and Ogbert and Wogmuth and Wigmund and Wagbert and—"

"You're just making them up!" said Charles.

"Of course I am. But they're names just the same."

Charles gave up. "All right, all right, get on with the case." And the questioning went on.

Simon was the last. Asked if there was any reason why he should not be sentenced, he said yes, there was, but that he had no objection to going to jail, so he would say nothing about it. "We've been living under the jail for some time," he said. "We have no objection to moving up one story into the jail itself. It's a pretty good place, from all

I've heard, and you'll have to feed us. I don't see what you gain by sending us there, but that's your affair."

"There's one thing we gain," said Charles. "We have had a good deal of trouble with the jail, I'll admit. Many animals have so good a time that they commit crimes just to be sent there. Some animals have even got in who haven't committed crimes or been sentenced at all. But Freddy has suggested a remedy. All sentences, from now on, will be *at hard labor*. There'll be no more playing games and carousing; the prisoners will work all day. The jail won't be so popular from now on."

The rats looked rather crestfallen at this. They whispered together for a minute; then suddenly, at a signal from Simon, they made a dash for the door.

They had been so reasonable during the questioning that even Jinx had been thrown off his guard. He made a pounce, missed Simon by the width of a whisker, then dove in among the legs of the audience after the fugitives.

"Let 'em go, Jinx," Freddy shouted after him. "Keep 'em away from the barn, but let 'em go!"

Jinx gave a screech to show that he had heard, and scrabbled on among the legs of horses and sheep and goats and all the other animals who had jammed into the cow-barn to hear the trial. Even outside, the crowd was thick, but he made his way as quickly as he could to the edge of it nearest the barn. Not a rat was in sight. "Lost 'em, by gum!" muttered the cat, but he went on cautiously toward the barn, from which came the sound of hammering. Evidently Mr. Bean was repairing the floor that the robbers had torn up.

"They won't dare go in that way," he said to himself. "This hole under the door is the most likely one. I'll watch that."

He crept up toward it and then, to his surprise, saw that a piece of tin had been nailed

across it. "Golly!" he thought. "If Mr. Bean
has found out about the rats, I'll be out of
luck. He must have, too, if he's found this
hole and nailed it up."

But there was one other hole on the other
side, so he went round to watch there. He
was pretty sure that the rats hadn't reached
it ahead of him. "If I can keep 'em out—"
he thought, and then he saw that the second
hole was nailed up too.

Inside the barn the prisoners, unaware of
the hard work in store for them, were singing and laughing and carrying on.

> "We raise our voices and shout," they sang,
> "And call the judge a good scout,
>   For he puts us in
>   And he keeps us in
>   And we'd rather be in than out."

Jinx grinned; then, as the song finished,
he heard someone talking. He stopped to
listen. ". . . didn't realize there were all
them rat-holes in the old place," Mr. Bean
was saying. "When I saw 'em, I was kind of

mad. 'Jinx ain't doin' his duty,' I says to my-self, 'to let them rats get a holt in here again.' But there ain't a rat in the place. I stomped all over the floor and took up a couple more boards and there wan't a sign of 'em. So I nailed up the holes, case any should come wandering along looking for a home."

"Oh, Jinx is a good cat," said Mrs. Bean. "He wouldn't let any rats get into the barn. Best mouser we ever had, Mr. B."

"You always *was* fond of that cat, Mrs. B.," replied her husband, "and I guess you been right. Takes a good cat to keep rats out of a barn with two big holes into it like I nailed up. Guess we might set him out an extra saucer of cream once in a while."

"I'll set out one for him this very night, Mr. B.," said Mrs. Bean. "What do you suppose all that rumpus is down at the cow-barn this afternoon?"

"Oh, another of their meetin's. I like to hear 'em shoutin' and bellerin' an' havin' a good time. I do hope they ain't goin' to take any more trips, though."

"You must 'a' read my mind, Mr. B.," said his wife. "But they're all taken up with this detective business now. That Freddy, he's a caution. Brighter'n a new penny! But then, so's Jinx."

"So's all of 'em, for that matter," said Mr. Bean. "There ain't a finer lot of animals in New York State, if I do say it myself."

Jinx crept away. He was a very happy cat. All his difficulties had been solved at once. The jury had declared him innocent, and the rats had been shut out of the barn. Lucky the trial had been going on while Mr. Bean nailed up the holes, or he'd have nailed 'em inside, and then there *would* have been trouble. But everything was all right now.

That evening he and Freddy and Mrs. Wiggins sat down by the duck-pond, watching the moon come up. The water rippled white in the moonlight—just the color, Jinx thought, of fresh cream.

"I've been working pretty hard the last few weeks," said Freddy after they had discussed the day's happenings. "I think I'm going to take a little vacation. Like to get off somewhere where it's quiet and there's nothing to do but loll on the grass and make up poetry."

"I'm tired, too," said Jinx. "All this rat business has got on my nerves. What do you say we take a little trip?"

"I think that's a good idea," said Mrs. Wiggins. "I can look after the detective business while you're gone, Freddy."

Freddy yawned. "Sure you can," he said. "Gosh, I hate to think of going back to that office tomorrow morning and interviewing clients and figuring out cases. Funny how tired you get of even the things you like to do."

"Like watching for rats," said Jinx. "I know."

"The open road," said Freddy dreamily.

261

"Remember that song I made up about it when we were going to Florida?"

"You bet I do!" said Jinx. "Let's sing it, out here in the moonlight."

"It's a travelers' song," said the pig. "Ought to be sung when you're *on* the open road; it's sort of silly to be singing it when we're sitting here at home."

Jinx jumped to his feet. "Well, *there's* your open road." He pointed dramatically toward the gate, whose white posts glimmered in the moonlight.

Freddy stared at him for a moment; then he too jumped up. "You're right," he said. "What are we waiting for? Let's go!" He turned to the cow. "Good luck, Mrs. W. Expect me back when you see me, and not before."

Mrs. Wiggins watched them go through the gate and off down the road together. Long after they had disappeared, the sound of their singing floated back to her through the clear night air.

Freddy sings:

O, I am the King of Detectives,
  And when I am out on the trail
All the animal criminals tremble,
  And the criminal animals quail,
For they know that I'll trace 'em and chase em
        and place 'em
  Behind the strong bars of the jail.

Jinx sings:

O, I am the terror of rodents.
  I can lick a whole army of rats
Like that thieving, deceiving old Simon
  And his sly sneaking, high squeaking brats.
For I, when I meet 'em, defeat 'em and eat 'em—
  I'm the boldest and bravest of cats.

Both sing:

In our chosen careers we'll admit that
  We haven't much farther to climb,
But we're weary of trailing and jailing,
  Of juries, disguises and crime.
We want a vacation from sin and sensation—
  We don't want to work all the time.

263

And then they broke into a verse of the marching song that they had so often sung on the road to Florida.

Then it's out of the gate and down the road
   Without stopping to say goodbye,
For adventure waits over every hill,
   Where the road runs up to the sky.
We're off to play with the wind and the stars,
   And we sing as we march away:
O, it's all very well to love your work,
   But you've *got* to have some play.

Mrs. Wiggins hummed the tune to herself for a while in a deep rumble that sounded like hundreds of bullfrogs tuning up. Then with a long sigh she got up and walked slowly back to her comfortable bed in the cow-barn.